ENTER
CLIFTON COUNTY

JULIE ANN FRANCES

PAGE PUBLISHING, INC.
Conneaut Lake, PA

First originally published by Page Publishing 2021

ISBN 978-1-6624-4329-9 (pbk)
ISBN 978-1-6624-4330-5 (digital)

Printed in the United States of America

Credit for cover photo:
Cover photo:
Julie Ann Frances/"Hampton"
Karen Taylor/"Hampton"
Special Thanks to the Dan Taylor Family

2022

Wishing you
a happy ever-after!

Jill Ann Frances

For Betsy

CONTENTS

Introduction...9

Enter Clifton County...11

Note to Readers...13

Chapter 1...15

Chapter 2...20

Chapter 3...25

Chapter 4...28

Chapter 5...32

Chapter 6...38

Chapter 7...42

Chapter 8...48

Chapter 9...52

Chapter 10...54

Chapter 11...56

Chapter 12...58

Chapter 13...68

Chapter 14...72

Chapter 15...75

Chapter 16...77

Chapter 17...80

Chapter 18...83

Chapter 19...86

Chapter 20...93

Chapter 21...99

Chapter 22...103

Chapter 23...108
Chapter 24...113
Chapter 25...116
Chapter 26...118
Chapter 27...121
Chapter 28...124

INTRODUCTION

As it goes with snowflakes, no two love stories are alike. And yet the settings for these fabled tales can be places where little ever changes except for the slow-rolling seasons. Enter Clifton County. On second thought, you had better jump in, because you do not want to miss a chapter or a season of this fast-moving love story.

Enter Clifton County

In south central Ohio, farm country, beautiful country, enduring, historic, patriotic, hardworking, and peaceful country, there is a sign on a state route that runs through some nice antique villages, past a huge man-created lake, hundreds of farms, and a dozen or so state preserves, rivers, fields, and ancient churches with ancient graves, testifying to the people who made the whole thing happen long ago. As you meander along and think you are in the most boring place in the world, you may see a sign ahead that says, simply, "Enter Clifton County."

Not "Welcome to Clifton County," not "Now Entering Beautiful Clifton County," just "Enter."

So then you know where you are. You might not want to enter, but if you do, you might not want to leave.

Note to Readers

Enter Clifton County by Julie Ann Frances is an original work of fiction. Any resemblance to any person (living or dead), place, thing, or event is unintended and coincidental.

CHAPTER 1

Vin Fackler did not go to the event that night to pick up a girl or even to watch them.

He went because he had to—was asked to—by his boss, Sheriff Earl Bittern, who was also his best friend.

It was one of those perennial fundraisers that seemed to increase in frequency and lack of imagination as times got pretty tough in Clifton County, a vast Midwestern farming community where prices of nearly everything needed to sustain a farm kept going up and raw crop prices kept going down. Beef and hogs had held that past year, but feed for the beasts had been almost enough to drive every farmer except the ones with steel tentacles to try chickens, designer herbs, or to just try another line of work.

Compared to the rest of the country, the price of acreage was good in Clifton County, and there was a lot of it, land which would probably never see a plow again. Many of the older family farmers and their farms did not continue after the current owners passed away, and foreclosures made for so many boarded-up, decaying houses and huge empty barns, it was hard to keep track of all of them.

As always happens, criminals took advantage of the vacancy situation and set up drug operations, methamphetamine labs, and marijuana fields out where they calculated no one would know, and often by the time the department was on to them, they were gone.

Vin had always found that criminals are easy to outsmart once you know what they are up to. But it was hard to find all of them in a place where there were hundreds of thousands of acres, mostly uninhabited by humans.

Folks, good folks, waited for things to get better.

Vin thought that Midwesterners probably were the most patient humans on earth. They were always waiting for things to get better, and if they didn't, the folks waited some more.

They waited for the package distribution air hub to come back. They waited for the oft-promised dispatch business to finally take over the land they had bought out on the highway. They waited for stores to reopen. They waited for the crops to grow. They waited for the weather to either get cooler or to get warmer, depending upon the season.

They waited for deer season. They waited for football season. They waited for the Reds to go to the World Series and for the Bengals or Browns to go to the Superbowl. They watched any kind of basketball all winter.

And always, always, nearly all of them waited for the team from Columbus to play football. The first football game of the season and the beginning of basketball season helped the local bars and restaurants fill up and keep a regular clientele throughout the fall and winter. The college was so massive and so much money and talent was put into the sports programs that the fans were rarely disappointed.

While the fine folks of Clifton County waited, some things just needed to be taken care of, which was why Vin was sitting in a bar at a fundraiser.

Clifton County had a fund-supported program designated to help the growing number of poor kids have new school clothes and a complete assortment of new classroom supplies for the annual first day of school, the feeling being that if a kid felt confident and ready for work on the first day of school each year, something good might follow. Local law or county accompanied the kids one on one at the mega mart, where they picked out a new suit of clothes and a new pair of shoes and looked around and just talked. Vin was one of the cops who did believe that even the short time anyone in a law enforcement uniform spent with a fully attentive kid who was fully attentive to him worked to help the kids understand that policemen were not just about shooting people.

He actually enjoyed those brief meetings with the kids, and he always took his own boys along for the experience.

At the registers, there were folks from Children's Social Services who let each kid pick out a new backpack, and the packs were full of school supplies, and the supplies were donated from the local citizenry and with funds from events like the one that night.

Vin always felt that schools should go back to a single pencil and paper system and give up all the electronic wonders and unions. He was an eight-crayons-to-a-box fan, and he thought that spell-check should be the job of a teacher with her hair in a bun, an apple on her desk, and a flowered cotton dress. He wasn't old enough to want black chalkboards to come back, but he could not understand what was wrong with a chalkboard of any color. A kid could get a temporary high sniffing correction fluid, but sniffing a black felt eraser did not produce the same effect.

He also thought that Ohio should be allowed to do what they wanted with their own schools. The success was there. Ohio had more universities than most other states, and if Kansas or Mississippi or California wanted to try other things, that should be left up to them.

His own boys had what they needed and most of what they wanted because he wasn't in the house to argue with them anymore, but when they were with him, they knew not to break out the electronic things.

Divorced for the third year, the father of two teenaged boys was finally over the time of his life when he needed counseling, a lot of alcohol, his best friend, Bitty, next to him at the bar, and the feeling of hanging on so tightly that he wanted to let go.

Joan had simply sent the boys to her parents one weekend and told him she was seeing someone new and she wanted him to move out.

Just like that.

All in one second, Vin had gone from loving his routine life with his job, his house, his truck, his wife, and his two kids to having nothing but his job and visits with his kids, and Joan wanted a major cut of his income. He got to keep the truck, but that was about it.

The papers had already been drawn up. He hadn't suspected a thing. If the boys had known, they never let on, and he never asked them. Betrayal from Joan was one thing, betrayal from his sons would have been quite another.

He tried never to think about that Saturday when he called Bitty, who came and removed his service revolver from the house and said nothing at all to either Joan or Vin. He had blocked the next hours of horror from his mind and only remembered them a little when he walked into his small apartment after his shift each day and had flashbacks of missing his house and his sons.

He was getting better about seeing Joan and her new husband when he picked up the boys every other weekend and the few discussions they had about the lives of the sons they had made together, and he no longer considered himself a part-time parent.

As much as he detested kids misusing cell phones, he made sure the plan he had with the boys was updated and paid, and he spoke with them every day.

Anyway, he had long ago lost the battle about school supplies, and if the sheriff wanted the deputies and their wives and girlfriends to come to a bar and eat and drink as a fundraiser, that seemed like a fair compromise.

Vin always came to these things alone.

Only a select few called Sheriff Earl Bittern "Bitty." There was absolutely nothing small about the man except for his height. In nearly twenty years working for Clifton County, Vin had never known another individual with the ironclad courage and will of Bitty, or the intelligence and cleverness it took to outsmart both criminals and politicians, which he had often confided to Vin were much of the same character.

He was the best of a best friend, and they had known each other since kindergarten. Vin and Bitty had shared a career and all the joys and sorrows of growing up, finding girls, marrying the right one, having kids, and raising them in a world where the law wasn't always black and white.

They had gone to college together, the academy together, and been hired together. They had been in the army reserves for six years together. Bitty had sought higher positions within the force, and Vin had not. They had each served as best man at the other's wedding. Bitty had three beautiful daughters, and Vin had two sons.

Bitty had the faithful and lovely Eileen, and Vin no longer had what he had thought was the faithful and lovely Joan.

Bitty moved in and out of the politics and realities of his job as head of more than seventy-five deputies, including six canines, and the administrator of the new facility he proudly called his jail, and about 90 percent of the time he kept smiling and made it look easy.

If there was a serious situation, Bitty was there, fully equipped and ready to back up any officer or squad who needed an extra hand. He went on regular patrol now and then, chased down an occasional runner just to see if he still could, threw down an occasional resist, escorted an occasional shoplifter to a cruiser, and drove him or her to his jail by himself. He had a particular affinity for orchestrating large drug busts, he liked to gather the outstanding warrant offenders all at once with his elaborate sting operations, and he eliminated a few prostitution rings, which always produced a lot of laughter but a lot of respect for Bitty in the report room at the beginning of each shift the day after a very difficult night.

Tonight he sat at a table with a couple of people from the Children's Social Services and Eileen and encouraged his deputies to donate some of the money they worked so hard to keep.

Eventually he approached Vin at a small table where Vin sat happily alone, sipping his beer and watching a basketball game.

CHAPTER 2

"You don't have to marry her. Just ask her for a date."

"What?" Vin was jarred from his peaceful solitude as Bitty pulled up a seat and sat across from him.

"I've been watching the same as you have… She's alone," Bitty said with a smile and a reassuring tone.

Vin sighed. Bitty knew him just well enough to have observed that while Vin watched the game, he was also watching a very pretty patron flit like a hummingbird from table to table, dancing as she stood in place and laughing and joking with people she knew.

It took Vin back to the days when he and Bitty were both single and constantly were on the lookout for girls each thought might be good for the other.

"Damn. Can't a fella just sit and watch a game? Did Eileen send you over here? I'm spending money. Isn't that why I had to come here tonight? Hell, I even took a shower," Vin complained.

Bitty did not stop his I-know-what-you-are-doing grin.

"She sure is pretty. I'm not even sure she knows it. Maybe you ought to go tell her."

Vin made a scoffing sound. "Sure. A girl like that wants an old, hard-ass, divorced son of a bitch like me to ask her to dinner. Sure."

Bitty stood up and pressed his palm into Vin's shoulder.

"Well, no one else is asking, partner! Shame to let an opportunity like her go down the drain to a lesser man!" Then he grinned again and returned to his table.

When Vin glanced at Eileen, she was looking at him and pushed her chin forward as if to say "Go on!" Vin frowned at her.

Collusion. They were in it together.

Vin looked for the girl. She was at the jukebox, tossing her hair out of her eyes and dancing a little, shifting her weight from foot to foot as she tried to pick songs.

Bitty was right: she was alone. Vin had been watching, too, so apparently he was interested. He was still contemplating his next move, if any, when all of a sudden the chorus of the song that was playing made nearly everyone in the bar chime in and move to the music, and when the girl started to wiggle a little more, Vin was practically catapulted out of his chair.

He couldn't feel his feet on the floor as he walked toward her. Then he was next to her, and he had to act.

"Hi! Do you need more money?" he asked, then immediately regretted it as a dumb thing to say.

The girl looked at him, amused. Up close she was even prettier, and the jukebox lights shot red and blue and gold fireworks through her chestnut hair. Her eyes could have been any color in those lights.

"Umm, no. I don't need more money." She smiled up at him and then looked back at the screen. "I just can't decide what to play!" She shrugged her shoulders, and her breasts jiggled.

Aw, come on! Vin nearly shouted. That was just so unfair, her breasts jiggling and him unable to openly stare at them. Before he undid himself by drooling and stuttering, he made a suggestion. A musical one.

"Didn't think of that one! Love it." She smiled at him again.

"How about if you play it and join me for a drink?" He tried to sound casual.

She shrugged again as she located the song he had suggested and pressed the combination of letters and numbers that would make it happen.

"Okay," she said with a smile.

Vin took a step back and gestured toward his table. Wordlessly and amazingly, the girl moved in the general direction where he ushered her without touching her. He pulled out a chair and sat down across from her, catching Bitty and Eileen's apparent approval from across the way. He rolled his eyes at them.

He ordered the beer the pretty girl, now amazingly enough seated across from him, wanted plus a glass and another beer for himself. It was then that he got a really good look at her, and something in his mind started to both amuse and warn him about her.

They had met before.

One household chore Vin had never reconciled after his separation and subsequent divorce from Joan was laundry.

He had a washer and dryer in his apartment, but it seemed more efficient to take the towels, bedding, and his uniforms and clothes to a Laundromat in Warmington. That way, everything was washed, dried, and folded within an hour and a half once a week, start to finish.

Then he would drop his uniforms off at the dry cleaner to be pressed. Correctly. He did not even try to accomplish that task himself, although Joan had done it for years without complaint.

It was a boring but necessary thing probably all men hated, but the hours Vin sat watching the clothes spin in the dryers seemed like a great way to forget about everything related to work and think about his boys, sports, his plans to buy some land, his boat, and fishing.

But one Saturday morning the past fall, his mesmerized staring had been suddenly interrupted by a female patron who accosted him for no apparent reason.

"Cut it out!" she had demanded in a seething tone, speaking from between clenched teeth.

Vin sat upright in his plastic Laundromat chair.

"What?" he replied, startled. "Cut what out?" He had frowned at her.

"You're staring at my underwear!" She jerked her head toward the wall of dryers Vin was facing. When he looked, he caught a quick glimpse of a hot-pink bra rotating in the glass dryer door.

Vin sighed and relaxed a little.

"No, I'm not staring at your underwear," he said simply.

"Yes, you are! And if you don't stop, I'm going to call the cops, you pervert!" she seethed.

That might have been interesting. And embarrassing. Vin looked again, and a pair of purple underpants was waltzing with some kind of ribbony thing in the glass. He quickly looked away.

He stood up, which put him at a nonthreatening but psychological advantage over her.

"Ma'am, I assure you I am not watching your underwear, or even my own. I am just staring into space here, okay?"

She backed down, but just a little.

"I know what you are doing!" she said, but a little calmer. She nodded as if to confirm her belief was valid. "Just cut it out!" she demanded.

Vin shook his head and sat down in a chair facing the washers. It seemed safe enough.

Eventually the girl removed her dancing unmentionables from the dryer and left the store. She had glared at Vin the whole time she assorted and folded her clothes.

This incident left his mind except to give him an amusing second or two every time he returned to the Laundromat after that day.

"I think I have seen you before," the girl across from the table beat him to the punch.

"Really? Where?" Vin tried not to laugh.

"Ummm…I don't know… Do you get your drugs from the Well Store in Hebron?"

He hoped she meant prescriptions.

"No, I like to confine my drug purchases to local dealers," he teased.

"Oh, I thought maybe you are one of my customers."

"Let's start at the beginning," Vin suggested. "I am Marvin, Vin Fackler." He held out his hand to her.

"Kerry." She accepted his hand, and they touched each other. She was soft and had lovely hands, a blue-stone ring on her right hand, no ring on her left hand, and pink nail polish. "Kerry Court."

She smiled right at him and Vin almost went blind.

"And I am a pharmacy technician," she giggled and jiggled, "not a drug dealer."

"Well, that's a relief. Have you figured out where you saw me before?"

She took a sip of her beer, which she drank from a glass. Like a lady, Vin noted.

"Nope! It seems like it was in a store, or a building…" She frowned and was still pretty.

Vin smiled. "Could it have been in the Laundromat on Central?"

He stared at her intently, still smiling, and watched her pretty face go from confusion to certainty to horror to embarrassment.

Kerry gasped. "Oh no! You're…you…," she stuttered.

"The Dryer Pervert." He put his hand out again. "Deputy Vin Fackler. Clifton County Sheriff's Department. Least likely tendency toward perversion in the state and maybe in the country."

Kerry groaned and laughed at the same time. She gave him her hand again.

She tossed her head, giggled, jiggled, took another sip of beer, and said, "It never fails. I do stuff like that all the time."

And with that, the ice was permanently broken.

CHAPTER 3

For a man who hated small talk, Vin sure drummed up a front loader full that night.

It turned out Kerry had a daughter at state, who had just bought her first series of student football tickets. Kerry said she hoped to go to a game in the fall and said she absolutely loved college football, high school football, and professional football if nothing else was on TV.

Game on, thought Vin. A woman who liked sports even a little was a good bet.

She was at the fundraiser because she gathered school supplies at clearance prices from the store where she worked and donated them to the annual drive. Her great-uncle was Tony, who owned Milo's, the bar where they were that night.

Tony was the man who coughed up proceeds from food sales for the county charities on a regular basis using nights like that one for events.

Vin did not tell her that as part of the divorce settlement, his attorney had managed to get him the former couple's season tickets to her daughter's school. They had been passed down to him from his parents when they just got too old to attend before his mother passed away. He would wait until he was sure they would be dating in the fall before he lured her with that prize.

When she told him where she lived, he swallowed a little. Kerry was the lone occupant of the impossibly huge maintenance monster of an antique house all the way out on the west end of the county. In fact, she lived in the first house inside that limit.

He had never understood why the guys had referred to it as the Baby Dream House over the past couple of years, but now he understood.

The house was beautiful, but he had heard deps tell of sitting entire nights chasing cattle and horses off the road, which for some reason wandered at night and just loved to go to that house.

They had been called numerous times simply to answer her front door in the middle of the night, which was their rule since the house had been involved in several incidents prior to her occupancy. It set back several hundred feet from the road, and the occupant or occupants were sitting ducks if anyone wanted to cause them trouble. People pulled off the road all hours of the night, usually to inform the occupant that her horses were wandering around, and since the current owner had no horses, some help was needed to get the damned things off the road and into a safe place.

The entire house had more glass windows than wooden walls, old glass that played with headlights and made them look like flashlights inside the house, with unlikely ghosts and possible criminals sneaking into and out of the high-ceilinged rooms.

The damned thing had three stories and a tower with long windows on all four sides. It had enough hidey-holes, staircases, and closets to require a canine unit to clear it, which had also happened once or twice.

Over the years, the house had few occupants and had been empty more than lived in.

Vin had never heard any of the guys describe the current occupant, and now he knew why: if Bitty or any of the sergeants knew there was a lone pretty woman at the house, they might have sent the younger officers there sparingly.

He told her that the west division of the county was not his patrol.

Kerry smiled a flirty smile, tossed her hair a little, and said, "Oh, that's too bad!"

She only drank one more beer and said she had to be at work in Hebron at eight in the morning. He understood. A twenty-year-old would have kept on drinking, but a fortyish needed some sleep.

It took absolutely no hesitation at all for Vin to ask her if she wanted to have dinner on Saturday night.

Kerry accepted with absolutely no hesitation at all. She said she had to work, but her shift was over at four thirty, and she was usually home by five and could be ready by six.

The deed was done. He hoped Bitty and Eileen would be happy.

"It's supposed to be really warm this weekend," Kerry said. "Maybe I can wear something not like a sweatsuit and a squall coat and we can find a patio. Wouldn't that be nice?" she asked Vin.

"Yes, that would be really nice, Kerry," he responded, noting that he had not spoken to anyone so softly for a long dry spell. They set the time.

He walked her to her girl car in the parking lot, waited as she snapped herself into her seat belt, and told her to drive safely.

"Sure!" She smiled that pretty smile at him, as he looked most of the way down her shirt from his position standing over the open driver's window. Then he stepped back as she backed out, looked both ways before she entered the same highway she lived on, and drove into the night.

He automatically recorded the plates in his mind.

Vin watched the car the whole way until the taillights disappeared. He felt great.

When he went back into the bar, there was a round of applause for him from his coworkers and from his boss, who had apparently been watching the couple the whole time. It was damned embarrassing, but he shook his head and smiled just a little, cashed out, and went home.

He hoped the fundraiser had been a success, because he certainly felt like a winner.

CHAPTER 4

Vin was glad there was only a short day and night and part of another day before he would pick Kerry up for their date, because maybe she would not have time to reconsider, and she did not have his number anyway.

Plus there was the plain fact that he thought about her and the upcoming date all the time when he was not involved in pure business.

One thing about being a county deputy, which Vin had always enjoyed, was that the calls didn't come right on top of one another, usually, and there could be a lot of wait time in between activities. There was plenty of time to think about a new lady, the future, a problem, or just about anything while you tried to think of what your next work-related move should be.

The deputies were free to drive around or just sit in one place for long periods of time and observe for speeders along the many county front and back roads. They were able to check on non-911 calls to help solve a problem or at least start a course of action, which would help a resident who had no close neighbors.

Things could happen to folks and property away from public sight, and no one would know. Bitty had no problem at all with his officers doing a little public relations work and checking up on the residents. In southern Ohio, a check on the welfare of the citizenry could often lead to some valuable conversation, some coffee and cake, or some lemonade, too. The longer he talked to folks, the more he learned about them and their situations, and it nearly always helped somewhere down the line.

If the department needed access to some remote area, which could only be reached by a private farm road, they did not usually have to ask permission. If a resident of a farm called and said they had not seen their neighbors for a while, a deputy could poke around and even enter the premises to check on welfare and not have to deal with the repercussions of activities on private property if he had made prior friendly contact.

Storm damage often left people in remote areas with no electricity, and many of the older folks did not have cell phones. They could be pinned under debris or otherwise impaired, and no one at all might know it for days. The older folks, many of them lifetime farmers, did not see the need to call for assistance if they had no heat or a way to get out for food. They tended to stay in their homes until they died, which was another problem because when they got sick, they often refused to seek care because they didn't want to be sent to a nursing home.

Roaming livestock that wandered onto the roads was another county problem. A semi driver with a full load traveling even at the posted speed had no chance to stop for a horse standing in his lane on the other side of a rise. Such a collision caused a not-always instant death for whatever beast meandered into disaster, and it often caused injury to the drivers, plus made the tractors undriveable.

In his entire career, Vin had never shot and killed a suspect, but he had shot and killed many a cow and two horses that had been not-quite-dead on the road, and it had not been pretty. Putting a maimed deer out of misery was frequent and an unsalvageable dog with no tags and no known home often met the same fate.

That kind of crisis with ensuing traffic jams on the two-lane roads required professional skill to safely reduce them and could take hours to fully resolve. The front loader brought in to carry away a mutilated horse or cow carcass, and either the coroner or a medevac to take away a human being were always the worst parts to witness.

And a car smacking into a deer could be a major incident. People who lived in the area rarely hit them since they constantly watched for them and drove just a little slower to avoid them, but the inexperienced usually found out about the nocturnal street-crossing habits of a deer the hard way, especially during rutting season, when the bucks spent twenty-four hours a day trying to sniff out the does and impregnate them.

The only good part about hitting and killing a deer on the road was that in Clifton County, the dead deer could become the possession of the driver if wanted, and there were several processing houses close by.

One December day, Vin had sent off a family in a sedan with a Christmas tree tied to the roof and a deer bungee corded to the trunk along with a mangled fender and grillwork. Their car told the whole story. It was one of the few visuals he allowed himself to recall.

Inside the city, there were warrants to be delivered and county and federal interventions to contend within the residential areas, and it seemed to Vin that these calls grew at an alarming rate.

Suicides were the worst, and they increased as the times grew tough. Getting a call to an old farm and having a distraught wife lead him to the barn, where she had just discovered her husband hung with his own belt from a beam, was hard to see. Finding a person of any age alongside a seldom-traveled road in a car who still had the pistol in his or her hand from a shot in the head left him at a loss for explanations.

There were sting operations that needed to be manned by county, and Bitty had a particular fondness for setting them up. If they were successful, and they usually were, he felt the need to call the television stations and newspapers and have his cleaned-up deputies stand in a line for a photo shoot the next day. They hated it, and Bitty knew this.

The sheriff also knew he could reward his hardworking, life-risking warriors with something as simple as free donuts or pizza, and they would stop complaining and move on to the next task.

Vin ate dinner with his sons that Friday night, and they talked about their upcoming spring break, which they would spend with him. They were still trying to decide if they wanted to go somewhere or just take the boat out on the lake, canoe on the river, go to the shooting range, maybe see all the movies their mother did not let them see, and just do local guy things.

They were good boys, Vin thought. In fact, they were great boys. Matt, the older at nearly sixteen, struggled in school but managed to get by with hard work. He was on the varsity wrestling team at the Warmington High School. The season had just ended, and he was just about dying to get a job, but knew he might have to give up other sports to do so.

Vin gave the boys an allowance as long as they stayed out of trouble and kept up their grades. He wanted them to work small jobs as he had done as a youth, but many of those jobs had disappeared as the economy worsened. Folks cut their own grass and shoveled their own snow. The boys lived too far away from the farms, where many chores were available. Even when they turned sixteen and were legally allowed to work, many of the jobs formerly filled by high school kids were currently held by adults as part-time second-job income for their families.

Mike, the younger of the two at fourteen, was a freshman and on the freshman wrestling team. He was an easy nearly straight-A student, belonged to every club he could join at school, could not get enough of his friends, and wanted to be a police officer of some sort when he grew up.

According to Matt, Mike had a girlfriend, so some discussion was needed about that, even though Mike denied anything but casual involvement.

I am going to have to practice what I preach, thought Vin when he spoke with the boys that Friday before his date. He chose not to tell the boys the old man was going out the next night.

CHAPTER 5

That Saturday, Vin finished his half-day shift at Bitty's jail, grabbed a to-go salad, showered, and got dressed for his date with Kerry.

He absolutely hated jail work, but he did it a few times a month and squirreled the money away. His regular salary and benefits took care of four people in two households, but Vin had always wanted a few acres of Clifton County to call his own and maybe a cabin or small farmhouse and barn to work on and play with. Plus he had two boys to send to college, and that wasn't cheap.

He was in line to inherit his father's farm one day, but the older man still farmed it practically by himself and rarely asked for help. He was in excellent health and intended to die in his fields one day, as was the usual intent of the Clifton County lifetime farmers.

Joan had never wanted some land. She wanted the money for a bigger, better house. She had taken half of that money and all of their house in the divorce settlement, but Vin had worked so much extra since the divorce that the amount was back to where it had been and then some.

Sometimes he and Bitty took pellet guns and walked land that was available. It was during these times that they talked about all things having to do with each other. They shot at rocks and fallen tree branches and made note of any place where they found evidence of a campfire or maybe some kids drinking illegally to have deputies watch for trouble.

Mostly they looked for stills and methamphetamine operations tucked back in the woods.

The extra money had paid for Vin's modest fishing/waterskiing boat, which he stored at his father's house. He took the boys a few vacation places, nothing terribly exciting, and he was saving in a separate account to buy Matt a small truck when the boy earned his license.

Vin almost laughed out loud as he struggled with the decision of what to wear for his date. They had not decided upon a place to go, so he did not know what Kerry expected. "Dinner" could cover a lot of outfits.

In the end, he chose a newer pair of jeans and a long-sleeved shirt. The weather was unseasonably warm, as Kerry had hoped, but he took along a light jacket since night still came early and the warm could go away.

He wanted to go to a nicer bar, or at least a place with a lot of televisions since the basketball playoffs were in full season, but he would do whatever Kerry wanted. After all, she was practically doing him a favor and certainly doing him the honor of even being with him at all. She was that pretty.

Vin drove past one of his own guys on the way to Kerry's house and was happy to be off duty that night.

When he thought about it, it had actually been about twenty-one years since he had a first date. His last first date had been with Joan, and after that date, he never even looked for another girl. He was glad he could think about Joan calmly at last, without the bitterness that had clouded his life in the past couple of years.

Vin was still moving on, but at least he was moving in the right direction.

As he drove down Kerry's driveway, he thought about the impossibility of her house. He decided she was either terribly romantic or terribly crazy. He would soon find out which one.

He knew to pull around the back of the house from having been there to remove hunters once or twice. So he stopped and parked the car, nervous as hell, took a deep breath, and got out.

Before he went up the steps to the back porch, the door opened, and a massive dog bounded out, rounded his truck, and leaped upon him.

"Geez!" Vin shouted, grabbed the dog in a bear hug, and proceeded to have his face licked enthusiastically, which was better than having it torn off.

"Oh my!" he heard Kerry before he could see her come to his aid. She shouted something, and the dog dislodged himself from Vin and ran to her. He seated himself in front of her, looking intently at Vin.

Kerry giggled as Vin tried to brush half of the dog off his clothes, which up to that moment had been clean.

"I'm so sorry!" she said from the porch. "I didn't know you were here!"

Hell, it was time for him to be there, Vin thought. When he looked at her, his temporary anger disappeared, because up to that moment, he only remembered what Kerry looked like in the dim light of the bar and the darkness of the parking lot.

Standing on her porch in the sunlight, she was dazzling.

"Hi!" was all he could come up with. He remained by his truck as Kerry had not invited him to come inside the house with her, and the dog pretty much did not want him to move a muscle.

"I'll get my sweater!" she said, opened the door for the beast, and disappeared, but while she had her back turned to Vin, his heart sank and alarm bells went off.

Kerry's longish, fullish coffee-colored skirt was see-through from the back. He wasn't taking her anywhere unless she changed it.

Normally, a guy wants a girl to have see-through clothes or, even better, no clothes at all.

From the front, Kerry's outfit was modest and pleasing, but from the rear, a lightly veiled full view of her black thong underwear, if that's what it was, and her two pale bottom cheeks were visible, along with the parts of her thighs that met her ass.

The front of the skirt gathered and fell flat against the flat front of her stomach, but the back did not have enough fabric to overlap.

Vin did not know this lady well enough to know if she was wearing this peekaboo skirt on purpose or not. He did not know if she wanted to maybe entice him or if she wanted to entice all the men wherever it was he took her.

He knew he did not want to spend the evening glaring at gawkers or worse. There was plenty a bar fight started by a pretty girl in sparing clothes, and in his line of work, he couldn't take a chance on being a winner or a loser of such a confrontation.

Vin sighed and walked up onto the porch. He had a loose plan. If it didn't work, he was going home. Alone.

The door opened again, and Kerry waltzed out.

"Hey, Kerry," Vin said to her. She was close to him then, and he could smell her. It was wonderful. She looked at him quizzically.

"I had a hard day at work and I have a headache and I am exhausted. Is there any way we could dine in tonight? I know you wanted to go to a patio, but I will get us any food you want, and we might watch the game on TV later. Would that be all right if I promise to make it up to you?"

She did look disappointed, but quickly recovered. She tossed her pretty shoulders, her pretty face, and her pretty hair and said, "Well, sure! It's okay!" but she looked surprised, as if she didn't know what to do.

So she opened the door again, the dog exited, and she and Vin entered. Before he could take in the expanse of the tall ceilings and adjust to the dimness of the old house, Kerry bailed him out.

"Hey! I made some chili to eat all weekend and I have beer. Would that be all right? I have some chips and salsa and—" Vin stopped her in midbreath.

He took a step to her, held her upper arms in his hands, and kissed her on her forehead. The sweet move surprised both of them. Then he rubbed her soft arms gently and said, "That would be just great, and thank you!"

"Okay!" She smiled as he let her go. She directed him to the room where the TV, a large coffee table, and a couch were located, kicked off her shoes, and went to the kitchen after handing him the remote.

"Do you need some drugs for your headache?" she called from the kitchen. Vin chuckled and declined.

What an accommodating girl, he thought as he sat down and located the pregame on the television set. He was with Kerry, she didn't seem too upset, she was actually fixing them dinner, and Vin was ready for whatever else the night brought.

The chili was good. She said there was plenty more for halftime. She asked him if they could take a walk since the sun was still shining and the game was not starting for another thirty minutes or so.

She talked a lot, or maybe she was nervous, wondering why he did not take her out after all.

The beast, whose name was Luke, of all things, enthusiastically accompanied them along the road behind Kerry's acreage. The road eased off the highway and took a right turn behind her place and then took a left and went off into what she said was three hundred fifty acres. It was freshly plowed and about-to-be-plowed, good-smelling Ohio farm dirt, which ended at a woods farther off.

She explained that she did not own the land except for the frontage on her farmhouse, but that since all the farmers had to have her permission to get to their fields using her road, she could walk wherever she wanted.

Vin just let her talk and talk. He wanted to walk behind her and watch her skirt show, but he managed to walk next to her, throw sticks for the dog, and listen to her chatter.

On the way back, she said, "You don't say much, do you?"

The obvious answer was that she did not let a person slide a word in sideways, but he just smiled and said "Nope!"

She did not talk during the game except to make enthusiastic comments and cheer. She drank her beer from the bottle at home, and she was barefoot, and Vin found himself to be comfortable with her. But her lips unconsciously nursing the beer bottle were, at the same time, making him uncomfortable.

They talked during commercials, ate chili again at halftime, and Vin felt himself growing uneasy in a way he had not expected.

He wanted her in a way that first dates did not politely allow, and the only way he was going to be able to get by was to leave and start over the next time, out in public somewhere, so it was not this convenient and Kerry would not be this easy to get. Every move Kerry made was making it worse.

She had no idea. His concern about the skirt had been unsubstantiated, but even the memory of how it had presented to him was making him crazier.

So he joined her in the kitchen when she carried the empty plates and bowls to the sink. He went up behind the skirt and took her arms again. She turned around, and he was just inches from her lips. And there was the cleavage, daring him to dive on in.

"What?" she asked, confused for the second time this evening.

"Kerry, I have to go. The chili was great, the walk and the entertainment were great, and well, you are great."

"What? Is your headache back? I thought we were having fun! I thought—"

Vin shut her up with a kiss.

"None of that. It's just me, Kerry, I haven't been with a pretty woman like you for a long time, and I just don't know what to do. So I better go. I had better just—"

Kerry didn't let him finish.

"I feel the same way." She nodded. Then she smiled up at him, a different kind of smile.

"I know what to do," she said in a low, seductive voice. She pressed her palms to his chest and pressed her lips to his lips and leaned in.

That was all it took.

CHAPTER 6

Vin never knew who won the game, and he didn't care until the next morning when Bitty suddenly called him and said he needed to see him right away.

Vin actually had made it home after an incredible time spent with Kerry, and he was grateful she did not beg him to stay in bed with her, because he would have done just that. Happily and forever.

Bitty was waiting at the donut shop near the bypass. He was not in uniform, and he was grinning as Vin joined him in the booth usually reserved for the sheriff, not by decree, but by local tradition.

Vin quickly determined that this meeting was not about police work. Bitty just looked a little too happy.

The server brought Vin's coffee without asking. And it only took a few seconds for Bitty to start in on him.

"Well?"

"Well what?"

Bitty thought for a moment.

"Who won the game last night, big guy?" He grinned.

Vin didn't know. So Bitty had him right where he wanted him.

Vin made a disgusted sound under his breath and bit into a donut, which he didn't even want.

"How was it?"

Vin put down the donut and pressed his back against the booth.

"You know, Bitty, some things a gentleman just does not discuss, even with his sheriff!"

"Ahh," said Bitty, "not true! My deputies have to tell me every-thing. How can I keep the peace in Clifton County if I don't know how they spend every waking, or sleeping, moment?"

Vin took a sip of his too-hot coffee and tried to look nonchalant as he burned his lips. Bitty waited.

"She was very nice…a very nice lady."

"A lady? That's good. Sometimes. Was she enough of a nice lady that you want to go back for more?"

"More what?" Vin pushed himself back from the table. "You know, Earl, if you want someone to talk dirty to you, why don't you try Eileen? Or maybe some of the women you are holding in your jail for solicitation? They might give you a freebie for a plea deal."

"Well, you don't have to tell me, I guess." Bitty backed down a little, and he seemed disappointed. "But you didn't know who won the game, so I just have to assume you were doing something more important than watching it. I can let it go at that. Are you going to ask her out again?"

Vin relaxed and finished the donut. He added ice from his water to the coffee and stirred it.

"Yes, if it makes your day complete, I would like to see her again."

"Oh, good!" Bitty grinned. "Eileen will be so happy!"

Vin cursed under his breath. He took a big drink of coffee, which was now too cold to enjoy.

Bitty noticed the subtle change in Vin and signaled for the server, who brought fresh coffee. Then the two friends talked about that game, the one Vin had missed, and the upcoming games. The sheriff was apparently satisfied with Vin's date as Vin was satisfied with his date.

Crazy satisfied. He was going to have to either stop over and see Kerry and leave his hands off her or call her and ask her out again.

He decided to go to her house after he showered, shaved, and redressed. By then he could have run her plates and obtained her phone number, and Bitty would have let him do that, but he didn't think it was fair for some reason.

When he got to her house, he realized that she was probably at work, which was good since he probably should have brought flowers. So he left a note with his phone number, waited, hoped, and at about five she called him.

It was almost like talking to a different person than the soft, determined, giving girl who he had spent half the night with.

She said they needed to talk, and then she started talking.

"You probably think I am a promiscuous whore," she stated.

"What? No! Not hardly!"

"Well, I never just jumped into bed with anyone in my life, at least not on the first date, which wasn't even a date, and you think I am easy."

"Stop!" he said simply, cutting her off midneurosis. He heard her suck in her breath and hold it.

"Kerry, I called to tell you that I had a wonderful time last night. And yes, things did move very quickly. But that does not make you whatever you called yourself, unless it makes me one, too.

"Men don't think like women do, Kerry. And we aren't sixteen or twenty or even thirty. I had a nice time last night, and I would like to see you again. I promise not to enter your house unless you want me to, and I absolutely will not make a move on you unless you want me to. I just want to have dinner. With you. Is that possible? I owe you dinner."

There was silence on the other end. Vin thought for a moment that she had hung up on him.

"Well, okay, I guess. But just dinner, okay?"

"Absolutely. How about in an hour?"

"Good."

"Okay," Vin said pleasantly. He hung up.

Geez, he thought. But really, he was sorry he had made her feel guilty. He certainly didn't share the feeling.

So the second date began with an understanding there would be no sex.

It didn't work.

They did have a really nice dinner at a steak house in Cincinnati with no television sets to distract Vin.

He had taken Kerry some violets, and she seemed truly touched, as the woman at the grocery store floral department had said a girl would be. When she put them into a vase and set them on her kitchen table, Vin thought he saw tears in her eyes.

They made it all the way back to her house after drinking a little at Milo's and talking for hours, and Vin walked her up on her porch, actually to make sure the dog was there, which meant the house was secure, and Kerry took him by the hand and pulled him inside after she shut the dog outside.

What was a guy supposed to do?

After that formal date, nothing either of them did prevented them from locking bodies at the end of subsequent dates. It became their first private joke.

Even mundane things like walking through the flea market for hours or antique shopping or Vin's introduction of the gun range to Kerry ended with sex.

Vin certainly had no complaints, and Kerry didn't either.

So within a month or so after their first date, they were officially seeing each other without ever having to say it.

Vin found himself in a relationship without ever having seen it coming, and Kerry said she had not been looking for anything so wonderful when she agreed to go out with Vin the first time he asked.

It was like taking a drive without either of them asking if they were there yet.

They were just there.

CHAPTER 7

Vin was actually driving toward Hebron when he got the call, an emergency call from work. He pulled off the road into a garden center.

"Deputy Fackler?" It was Bitty, and this was business.

"This is Fackler."

"There has been a holdup at the Well Store in Hebron. Armed robbery. No one is hurt, but the personnel are very shaken up. Local has the suspect. I wonder if you have time to see if he is anyone of interest to us? Get the info, and we can check for superior warrants."

Vin swallowed. Bitty was speaking in code. Kerry had just been held up at gunpoint, or at least was in the general vicinity of the robbery. Bitty was letting him go and take care of her and see the man who scared her too.

"I have my boys with me. We are near Hebron," Vin responded.

"Take them with you. Your role will only be to identify and photograph the suspect."

"I'll get right on it," Vin responded. He reached into his wallet, pulled out his badge, went to the trunk and holstered his service revolver, scared the hell out of the boys, and drove out of the garden center before he spoke to them.

He had not told them about Kerry. And today was not going to be the day if he could help it. Not in this situation.

Ahead on the road was a shopping center with a wings place the boys liked. There were video games there. He explained that he had to work for a little while and pulled into the wings place.

Vin got out of the truck and reached for his wallet, which was right under his gun. He saw the boy's eyes just about pop out of their heads.

He withdrew more than enough money for them and told them they could eat what they wanted and play games until they ran out of money and they had better not fight about it. He told them he would call them. He kissed each of them and watched as they walked into the restaurant.

Then he thought better of releasing two underage teens into a restaurant, so he dashed inside, showed his badge, and told the host that he had an emergency.

He smiled at the idea that the boys thought he was drawing his gun when he went for the money. He got back into the truck.

Not far ahead on the highway, he saw all the lights at the Well Store. Kerry's Well Store. There was a full complement of local and county units, and state patrol was running the traffic, directing folks to keep on going and not stop and gawk.

He showed his badge, and they let him through.

Vin parked on the side of the store and tried to think about what he could possibly say to Kerry about this. He thought maybe it would take care of itself. But first he needed to see that she was unharmed.

They let him in through the guarded, locked door and directed him to the office in the back behind the pharmacy. There he said for the first time that Kerry Court was his girlfriend.

It surprised him to hear the words come out of his mouth. They let him in.

Kerry was folded over in an office chair, trying to control her hysteria. When she saw Vin, she gave up. She ran to him and threw herself at him, and he had to hold her up.

He felt her strength and determined that she was all right, just terribly wronged and scared. She cried and tried to talk, and all he could do was hold on to her and stroke her hair and back until she slowed down a bit.

The pharmacist, John somebody or other, a nice guy whom Kerry liked to work with, was seated and filling out papers. He looked grim.

"I was in the bathroom. She had to handle it all by herself," he said quietly to Vin.

"What happened?" Vin said to no one in particular. A local officer, a sergeant, filled him in as Kerry was far from being able to talk.

So she had been working, and this bozo just waltzed in through the front door. He had a handgun, an automatic, already drawn when he came in. The cashier in the front was with a customer and did not see him. He made it all the way to the pharmacy in the rear of the store, displayed the gun to the hapless Kerry after waiting for her to finish with a single customer, then he aimed the gun right at her and told her to open the safe. He jumped over the counter to make certain she did not trip an alarm, which she already had done, a silent alert.

Then the pharmacist returned. The safe had been open, which was against company policy, so he was in some sort of trouble. The perp held the gun at the guy's head while Kerry unloaded pills into unlabeled vials from a carton near the safe on the floor. She had been in the process of putting away a shipment when the incident occurred.

Then she dropped the drugs into store bags and held up her hands as directed. The guy told her to open the register, and she did so, handing him all the paper money, just as the manager reached the area.

The perp waved the gun around and left the store, heard sirens, and took off in a waiting car.

At the next corner, cops tried to surround the vehicle. The robber jumped out and ran. The driver sped away, and there was no way to shoot out his tires as the area was full of traffic.

A canine unit got the runner, but the driver escaped with the goods.

"Kerry did exactly what she was taught to do. She gave the asshole everything he wanted. She did not argue, for once. I am proud of her," her manager said to Vin.

Yeah, thought Vin. It must have taken a boatload of fear to make Kerry not throw bottles or something at the guy or try something else.

The manager shook his head and looked toward the pharmacist, who was doing well considering he had just had a gun held to his head.

"We have to go do a count," the manager said to him.

"Narcotics," the pharmacist said to the roomful of law. "We should be able to know exactly what they got, including manufacturers, lot numbers, etc."

It was only then that Kerry spoke. She turned her face away from Vin's chest and said simply, "No need."

Everyone looked at one another.

"What do you mean, Kerry?" her manager asked, coming closer to her to hear her better.

Kerry straightened up then. She did not let go of Vin, but she turned around and accepted another tissue. She wiped her eyes, ran her fingers through her tousled hair, and spoke loudly enough for all to hear.

"He didn't get any narcotics. I gave him the stuff on the floor. He didn't see me switch it out because he was busy with John."

"What?" John said. If what Kerry said was true, the pharmacist was not only out of minor trouble, but he would not have to answer for the loss to the state narcotics board.

No controlled substances from that store would be out on the streets.

"What did he get, Kerry?"

Kerry stopped crying completely. For a moment, Vin thought she had lost it because she squared her shoulders and smiled a little.

"Estrogen. A lot of Estrogen. And ED tablets…all that was in the box."

"ED?" Vin asked.

Kerry turned to him. She spoke up so all in the room could hear her. "You don't know because you don't need them. Erectile dysfunction."

Vin blushed. Within seconds, everyone in the room was all smiles.

But before the jokes and congratulations were in order, Kerry and John and the manager had to identify the perp, who was dog bitten and complaining outside in a cruiser.

Kerry didn't want to do it. Vin had to do some smooth and insistent talking to get her to walk into the sunlight and see the perp face-to-face again.

She started to cry, but at least she wasn't shaking. She was just angry.

"I'm right here, and I won't let you go," Vin promised.

So he walked right behind her, and he just felt so sorry for her when she had to approach the cruiser and look at the guy, who was ugly, mad, and spit at her. He called her a bitch. Vin wanted more than anything to have just ten or fifteen seconds alone with the guy. Or even three seconds.

But Kerry surprised all of them again, including the perp.

"To hell with you!" she seethed. Then she repeated it, louder. She kicked at the cruiser. Vin turned her around and walked her back inside, knowing anger was better than fear in this case. It meant she felt safe enough and was ready to move on.

They let her go as they were closing the store for the rest of the day while the locals did their work. Her manager just wanted to know if she would ever come back. He gave her the next three days off. He looked at Vin, asked him to take care of her, and told him he needed her.

That made two of them.

Kerry got her purse, went to the bathroom, and rinsed her face with cold water, and she even brushed her hair and put on lipstick, a sign that a woman felt she would be all right. Then Vin took her out of the store to his truck. She didn't ask to drive her car home.

He almost forgot about his sons. He almost forgot to take the picture. He went back to the cruiser and took the best shot he could from an unwilling asshole in a police car. He didn't recognize the guy from anything in Clifton.

He thanked everyone before he returned to Kerry, who had already turned on the radio and looked like she had not a care in the world.

As Vin was driving out of the parking lot, though, she started to cry again.

"I needed you!"

He told her that he was sorry he wasn't there to help her, which was the pure truth. It was always nice to be needed.

Then he told her she was about to meet his sons.

CHAPTER 8

You had to know that Kerry had just been in a holdup to know how extraordinary it was for her to rise as she did to meet Matt and Mike.

If not for the red eyes and the pinker-than-usual cheeks and nose, Vin would not have guessed either.

The boys were certainly surprised to have their dad walk into the restaurant with a pretty woman who was not their mother, for which they had not been prepared.

Vin quickly introduced Kerry, said she was a friend of his, and told them she had been involved in the call he attended and what had happened. He skipped the erectile dysfunction part.

They fumbled a little and started to ask questions about what it was like to have a gun pulled on you, but Vin shut them up with a single look and an almost imperceptible shake of his head.

Kerry changed the subject and asked about the menu. Vin didn't really think she was hungry, but she needed to do something, so she picked up a menu and acted like she was interested.

The boys were not, of course, but they didn't argue about Vin buying more food and drinks.

"Dad, we have money left over," Mike offered.

"Split it up between you, son," Vin said. "And thank you for understanding why I had to go on the call."

The boys nodded. The reason was that their dad was dating and his date dated a policeman. They knew he was seeing someone, but having her here with them was definitely something new.

The conversations were a bit stilted. Kerry was not herself, understandably, and Vin was worried about her. He was afraid she would never go back to work.

He didn't know what he was going to do. Kerry needed him, really needed him, and he had the boys for the night. He wasn't going to take them home, and of course he didn't want them to know he was as involved with Kerry as he was, meaning that he slept with her.

So he called his dad and asked if he would keep them for the night. Of course the answer was yes, and he told the boys there had been a change in plans.

They adored their grandfather. It was no problem for them since they could see Kerry fading away as she sat and tried to eat. They were old enough to understand that she needed their dad more than they did for one night.

So they ate a little and boxed up the remainder of the food, and Vin drove them all to his apartment so the boys could get their clothes and toothbrushes and stuff, and then he drove them to his father.

Kerry ended up meeting Vin's father too. Vin briefed him, told him they had to pick up Kerry's car, go walk and feed her dog, and that he wanted to be with her for the evening. He was careful not to say "all night."

But his dad winked at him and told Kerry he hoped she would be all right and that he was sorry she had been through the holdup.

"That would scare the hell out of anybody," the retired cop said to Kerry.

Just before Vin got to his truck to take Kerry home, Matt called to him and ran across the yard to talk to him.

He directed Vin to join him out of Kerry's earshot.

"What is it, son?" Vin asked. With a sixteen-year-old boy, it could be just about anything.

"Dad, I know you are going to, umm, spend the night with Kerry. I won't tell Mike. Or Mom. If I had just been through what she has, or if Mom had...well, we would need you. All night. I don't want her to be scared. If you are there, she won't be."

Vin hugged Matt and kissed him on his neck.

49

"And if you want me to stay with her tomorrow night, I will."

"Thank you, Matt, for understanding. I don't want her to be afraid either."

Matt nodded and turned back for the house.

Vin sighed. What a moment, and what an afternoon this had been, he thought.

Kerry grew anxious as Vin drove closer and closer to her store. He asked her if she felt all right to drive, and he saw her nod out of the corner of his eye.

He walked to her car with her and told her he would follow her home, not the other way around. She didn't argue, which worried him just a little because Kerry liked to control everything.

She drove all right, but she sat just a little too long at a couple of green lights and made a right turn on red without looking. Fortunately, no other car was in the area at the time.

When she parked in her driveway, she did not get out of the car. She just sat there. Vin heard her beast barking hysterically inside, and he already knew the door was open, so he went up on the porch and let Luke escape into the early evening sun.

The dog did not give Vin a passing glance. He just went for Kerry.

Bingo.

Kerry opened her door and stepped out. Luke took over. No one could ignore and not get caught up in the dog's enthusiasm. Kerry held out her arms, and Luke gladly obliged, practically knocking her to the ground.

Kerry said, "Let's take a walk!" and off the dog ran, with Kerry following behind. She didn't call for Vin, so he thought maybe she wanted to be alone. He waited on the porch, where he could see the pair most of the way, and then he ascended the three flights of stairs and stood in the house's tower, where he could watch them as they went farther away from the house and returned again.

By the time they came back, Kerry seemed to have worked a few things out. Vin thought she probably looked around and saw that the country world she knew had not changed or even reacted to what had happened in any way.

He sighed. That was the beauty of Clifton County, with the vastness of rolling farmland oblivious to human concerns. There was a constant calm and a slow, steady progression of what occurred in the seasons and the times in between them, and that part never changed. Never.

The things people did to one another did not matter out here. Kerry's incident was not noticed by the fields, the birds, and the trees along her walk. Luke only knew that she was home and that his life had just improved.

And Vin knew that he was with her, and that when he was, he always felt wonderful. He would do whatever he could to help her get through this, and it started when he walked across the yard as she approached the house and he swept her up in his arms and carried her the rest of the way, making her throw her pretty head back in laughter.

CHAPTER 9

The next morning, with Vin needing to rescue his dad from the boys and also needing to stay with Kerry, Vin made a plan for the day and pretty much told Kerry what to wear, saying they were going to have fun all day.

She had slept most of the night. Next to her in her partly rusty antique metal bed, covered with the colorful patchwork quilts she had told him were made in the forties, Vin only slept halfway, wanting to be right there if Kerry had any sort of sudden fright or nightmares. She had awakened twice and reached for him, and when she knew he was there, she went back to sleep.

That was nice, to be needed like that by a woman, but he would gladly have traded it away for a normal day at work for Kerry the day before.

He walked the beast by himself, jogging and taking in deep breaths of the clean, fresh air as he threw sticks and stretched his underworked limbs.

When he got back to the house, Kerry had showered and was already mostly dressed, and he told her they were going to go to breakfast and take out his boat.

She wasn't thrilled, but she was okay with it.

Good enough, thought Vin. Usually, they did whatever Kerry wanted to do, which was always all right with him.

He took them all, including his father, to a breakfast buffet. They all ate and talked and talked and ate until it seemed no one could eat anything else or had anything else to say, which was what Vin wanted.

He invited his father to take the boat out with them, but the older man declined, and Vin thought he probably had enough of them for the time being. But he helped Vin and the boys uncover and pull the boat out of the pole barn where it had spent the winter, helped Vin hitch it up, and they started the motor a few times with fresh fuel and oil.

They took the boat out onto the lake. It was slow going because there was a lot of floating debris from the winter runoff and the day wasn't warm enough to want to have the air driven into one's skin with speed. But the lake was sparkling and dark blue, the underbrush and a few trees were practically glowing yellow green on the banks, the sun never stopped shining on them, and the boys were excited about the upcoming fishing season.

Back at Kerry's, the boys explored her crazy house after Mike asked if it was haunted, and they ran and romped with Luke, ate hot dogs from the first cookout of the season, and generally just had a nice, casual afternoon.

Kerry still didn't say much, and Vin thought she might be afraid about going back to work as the time got closer for her to engage again.

When he got the boys into the truck to take them home, she said she would be all right and that she would see Vin the next day.

He smiled at her as sweetly as he could, but his tone was very clear.

"I'm not leaving you."

She sighed but got into the truck for the ride.

CHAPTER 10

Morning report that Monday was nothing short of hilarious. Without giving Kerry's identity or her connection to the department away, Bitty himself addressed his deputies, displayed Vin's photo of Kerry's robber, and asked if any of them recognized him, and then he told the hilarious description of what they could look for if any of the users were in the area due to their inability to know that they had been duped.

Bitty made it quite clear that the symptoms he was about to describe came directly from a certified, registered pharmacist and that no sexism was intended.

His audience was all ears.

"Look for men with growing breasts and high-pitched voices who cry a lot. Those are the ones who think they bought Demerol but actually are taking large doses of estrogen. They might be asking strangers if their asses look too big. Look for men with, well, look for pole vaulters," he said dryly. "And those would be the users who are now frequently using the erectile dysfunction pills, taking more and more because they don't understand why their high is only in their pants."

Bitty had to wait for the laughter to die down a bit, and as usual, his comedic timing was perfect.

"And as for the women, they won't look any different," he continued. "Except they might get prettier."

Vin laughed so hard he almost cried. Even the female deputies found this twist to be the rare cause for the jokes they usually had to try harder to laugh at.

Bitty kept him up to date about the arraignment and plans for the robber, and he also kept Kerry in the know. Vin knew she was worried that somehow the perp would be let off, especially since he had not actually taken any narcotics or that he would be free on bail.

But she did not have to worry, at least not for months to come. The guy had such a long list of prior charges and convictions that Bitty spoke with the sheriff of Warner County, and he felt that this time, the prosecutor would go for some extended time in prison.

So Kerry went back to work. Construction was planned for a bulletproof shield to be installed across the entire pharmacy counter even though her manager really had to fight for it.

She told Vin that customers did not seem to understand that she did not want to discuss what had happened with them and she had asked John to keep her in the fill area, away from the service windows.

That seemed fair enough. Her manager was so happy she had come back that he wanted her to have anything she wanted as long as she was in the pharmacy.

Kerry was self-supporting, so she needed to work. There were signs all around that she barely earned enough to keep her head above water, but she had never complained, at least not to Vin.

CHAPTER 11

Kerry seemed to celebrate her paydays more than most people did. She and Vin drove to the mill in Warmington to pick up a fifty-pound bag of dog food for the beast every month, and she always made a show of his ability to easily hoist the bag and empty it into the bin she kept in her mudroom.

She would take on a comical Southern accent and say, "I declare! You are just the handsomest, strongest man, maybe in the whole county!"

Then she would flirt with him, gently squeeze his biceps, and croon sweetly, at which point Vin would usually pick her up and set her on her kitchen counter, tickle her a little, and make her giggle. Once he lifted her atop her refrigerator and she couldn't get down.

They drove all the way to a store in Franklin monthly to select really good meat for grilling or for Kerry to fix for him, and she always tried to pay for it, but Vin insisted that his meat was always free for Kerry. He said it every month, and she smiled and shook her head a little every month as if she had not heard him say it before.

He never saw her bills, ever. She took them from her mailbox on the road and put them somewhere to either pay them or worry about them, he never knew which.

He wasn't the kind of boyfriend who picked up her mail for her while she was at work as a veiled favor. No way would he invade her privacy like that.

She ran her car on empty, and every now and then, when she was at work and he was off, he took his ten-gallon can he used for the boat and filled her tank in the parking lot of the Well Store.

Then he would drive to the drive-through window and say hello to her, just to see her.

He kept her lawn tractor running, and he mowed her four acres every now and then, but mostly he let his boys do it, as they fought over what they considered to be the privilege. He wouldn't let her pay them, as they got an allowance, but he saw her slip them a few bucks every now and then when they completed the job, and he acted as if he did not see her do it.

The best thing Vin could think to do for Kerry was to kidnap the beast once every six weeks or so and drop him off at Eileen's dog grooming shop, where she worked wonders with the dog's craggy appearance. Eileen groomed all six of the county's canine units, and she did it for free, so as not to cause any conflicts for Bitty.

Vin paid her for Luke's improvements, but he thought Eileen probably gave him the Chihuahua rate.

Eileen instructed Vin to purchase prescription flea and tick medication from the department's veterinarian, which was expensive as hell, but better than having the dog fill Kerry's house, most importantly her bed, with parasites.

Kerry just assumed the medication was included with the grooming Vin paid for. Had she known, she would have put a stop to both the grooming and the meds.

CHAPTER 12

Easter was one of Vin's favorite holidays not because of chocolate bunnies or baby ducks but because Easter signaled the end of the cold, freezing weather, which made the job logistically harder.

It signaled the beginning of boating and fishing, the farms springing to life, and all the green, which made Clifton County just one of the most beautiful boring places on earth.

Wrestling and basketball ended, but baseball began, and so did training for the annual softball match between the local police and the deputies.

And that was serious business. The game was a fundraiser, but for all the participants, it was a game of pure pride. The constant jibes and snide remarks between them looked like fun to those who witnessed them, but there was an undercurrent of serious competition that was pumped up this time of year and crescendoed as the season progressed.

But there were seasonal trade-offs. The exit of snow and ice opened the door for warm-weather problems.

Spring tornadoes were a constant worry, but their actual occurrence was rare. And there was so much open space in the county that the occasional twister, which did touch down usually, didn't do much damage to structures.

But violent spring and summer storms were frequent, with wind shears up to a hundred miles per hour. After these events, deputies spent a lot of time checking on the remote residents.

When their phones went down or their electricity went out or a tree fell on their house or blocked their ability to exit their driveways they needed help, and many of the stoic Ohioans did not ask for assistance, especially the older farmers.

They were so used to taking care of everything for themselves, Vin figured, they did not see storm damage as an emergency situation.

And of course, trees fell on fence lines, and out came the cattle and horses, and it seemed to him they went right for the highways.

There was yet another annual fundraiser the Saturday before Easter, sponsored by the sheriff, children's services, and the local police.

It was held at the high school and played out as a carnival of sorts for the kids, since sometimes the weather was not so good for them to be outside much during their break from school.

The high school kids ran games, the funds bought some little prizes, and there were free hot dogs, lemonade, cupcakes, and a crazy Easter egg hunt all over the school.

The money was raised by pure "open your wallet and dump some money into the metal box at the door" and by ticket and snack bar sales from a basketball tournament.

But the best part was that every year, the loser of every single one-on-one creative game of skill the sheriff and the local chief could think up and bet upon went on for a month.

The overall loser of the final competition, a dart tournament at Kerry's uncle's bar, which was another fundraiser, had to dress up in a huge white fuzzy Easter Bunny suit and officiate at the kid's carnival. Since bunnies didn't talk, he had to remain silent for hours and take all the catcalls and insults without comment. Plus the suit was hot inside, and many of the kids had wet pants. And there were the screamers.

Bitty hated that damned bunny suit. He hated it more than he hated just about anything else. Nearly every time he was supposed to wear it, he had a last-minute all-or-nothing match, and if he won, his designated loser had to wear the suit. Usually no one challenged him, but that year, Vin got pretty drunk and took him on.

He lost.

The only person he told was Kerry, because he had to change their morning plans and start out in Warmington at the costume shop, which rented out the rabbit suit. Since there were only a few hours between the switch and the appearance of the bunny, no one needed to know, and they would all see Bitty furless and walking around the event anyway.

Bitty made Vin leave his truck at the bar and drove him home because he drank too much. Kerry had left earlier, saying she had to get a spring outfit out of storage and launder it, and she wanted to highlight her hair.

It was probably best that she deserted him, Vin had thought. He was in a bad mood after losing, and he might have not been so nice to her as she had been in a teasing mood that night.

Kerry could not have known that when Bitty picked Vin up in the morning to retrieve his truck, the lunch cook doing routine morning prep let them into Milo's and they had one more unwitnessed match. Vin said that Bitty had taken advantage of his drunken state and that he knew it.

And much to Vin's exquisite joy, Bitty lost, by about one thirty-second of an inch.

Sometimes life was just so sweet, Vin thought as he went back to his apartment, showered, and ate some eggs. He would see the boys at the event, Kerry would be there, and Bitty would be in the damned Easter Bunny suit, and all because of a single skilled throw of a dart.

He would not have to rub it in, either, because when the others saw him, they would know about the final switch. Many of them thought Bitty was in the suit anyway.

When he entered the event, Vin made a contribution and went right to the cafeteria, where the boys had said their clubs were working on the food and drink. He said hello to the boys and gave them a hug, and they said that Kerry was in the gym and that she looked really pretty.

Nice of them to notice, thought Vin.

She did look really pretty. She was wearing a flowered skirt, an opaque one, a pink sweater with another pink sweater over it, a pearl necklace, and earrings, and she just looked like a whole bouquet of flowers. He was pretty sure she smelled like one, too, and he was about to find out as he made his way through the crowded gym to see her and pay his respects to the Easter Bunny, which was going to be particularly sweet.

Vin was delayed by friends a couple of times, so he didn't see Kerry in the line to sit atop the bunny's lap, and when he did, she was next.

It was all too funny. Kerry was about to sit on Bitty's lap, thinking it was Vin. And since the Bunny couldn't talk, his secret was safe.

So he stood about thirty feet away, camouflaged by a large green plant festooned with plastic Easter eggs, and watched as his girlfriend climbed up onto his boss's lap.

He even took a picture with his phone.

Kerry leaned in and whispered something to the bunny, and she giggled a little, and the reaction of the bunny was comical. Bitty took both of his huge paws and pressed them to his cheeks and shook his head as if Kerry had said something shocking.

Then Kerry kissed his pink nose and hopped off his lap. Vin loved it.

He came out from behind the Easter Egg plant, or whatever it was, walked across the gym, and encountered Kerry at the lemonade stand.

"I saw you flirting with that damned rabbit!" he said from behind her.

Kerry turned around with a smile on her face, and then everything went terribly wrong.

She looked at Vin, looked toward Bitty, and looked at Vin again. Her mouth dropped open, and she shrieked a little then ran out of the gym.

The look on her face was of true horror. Vin was concerned enough to try and hurry behind her, but there were so many kids and folks in his way Kerry got to her car and was driving out of the lot before he could reach her.

She possibly didn't hear him shout at her to stop, and if she did, she ignored him.

Vin jumped into his truck and followed Kerry wishing he had a cruiser because she was definitely speeding. Once she got past a couple of red lights before the highway opened up and went straight to her house, he lost her. Two of them did not need to speed, he thought, and he knew where she was going.

The dust was still flying when he turned into her driveway. Her car was already parked, dumped, actually, in a corner of her yard, and she was on her side porch swing, crying hysterically. She was folded up like an origami flower. The swing was quivering. Luke was nowhere in sight.

"Kerry! What the hell was that?" Vin yelled at her as he approached, referring to her unsafe dash from the high school.

She didn't answer.

So he went up to the vibrating swing and just stood there for a minute, waiting for her to either speak or explode, she was so upset.

"Damn you!" she shrieked at him.

"Damn me? Not unless you tell me what I did!"

"You were sup...posed to...b-be the buh...hun...ny!" she sobbed.

He sat down next to her. If nothing else, he wanted the swing to stop shaking before it dislodged from the rotting roof of the porch.

"Oh, hell, Kerry! Is that what this is all about? Because I wasn't the bunny? I'll be the bunny next year, I promise!" Vin took his hand and stroked her shoulders and back softly.

Kerry turned halfway and slapped his hand away. She looked at him accusingly.

"I didn't know it wasn't you! I didn't know the bunny was the sheriff!" she tried to explain.

Vin still did not understand.

"Well, so what?" he tried to get more information. Kerry folded up into hysteria again.

Geez, Vin thought. This was harder than it looked. He touched her again, hoping to somehow soothe her. It had worked before.

Kerry slapped at him again, for no reason. So he just sat there.

Eventually, he thought, she would calm down and tell him what he had done, because he certainly had no idea. And she needed a box of tissues soon. Or a bucket to hang around her neck to catch all the drippings. She also needed to quit slapping him, not that it hurt.

After a few long minutes, she did calm down enough to talk. She sniffed and threw her hair back.

"I didn't know it wasn't you. It was supposed to be you!" she started. But what she thought was an explanation still made absolutely no sense to Vin.

She looked at him and saw the confusion on his face.

"It's what I said to him…to the bunny! I-I said—" Then she collapsed into hysteria again. "He's going to think I am a promiscuous whore!"

There were those words again, the two words Kerry used to damn herself and any other woman since time began whom she thought gave her body away a little too loosely.

"Okay, okay." Vin got serious and went into deputy mode, albeit a bit more gently than usual. "What exactly did you say to Bit…to the Easter Bunny, Kerry?"

She stopped crying completely and hung her head in shame. She waited a few seconds.

"First I told him I wasn't wearing un-un-underwear! Then I told him to come over later and we could play hide the carrot."

She collapsed into sobs again.

Did Kerry really say that? Vin thought to himself. This was absolutely too funny. And he did not dare crack a smile. Inside, though, his guts were quivering with wild laughter he did not dare express. He tempered his response with what he hoped was a caring tone.

"Well, that's no big deal. He probably didn't hear you in that suit. The head is thick and there are no earholes and—"

"He heard me," Kerry said sadly, calmer now, shaking her head. "He shook his head and put his paws up to his cheeks like he was embarrassed. I thought it was you, so I thought it was funny. He must have been shocked as hell."

Bitty shocked? Not likely, Vin figured. He was probably thrilled to death knowing Vin had a lady who liked to talk a little dirty, and who had just talked dirty to him.

"Well, Kerry, I know Bitty. I doubt very much he was shocked, and I know for a fact he does not think you are…whatever it is you called yourself. Men don't think that way, Kerry. He was probably flattered."

Kerry's head drooped farther and farther onto her chest. A couple of fresh tears actually splashed off the top of her breasts, which were very modestly tucked into the innocent pink sweater. Vin scooted next to her and put his arm all the way around her. He started to rock them in the swing. He leaned over her shoulder and kissed her on the top of her sweaty head.

"I can't ever look at him again," she said sadly.

"Now that's just not true. I told you men don't think like women do, Kerry, trust me on this one."

She shook her head, apparently unconvinced. But she had stopped crying, stopped slapping at him, and stopped violently shaking, so she was getting over it.

Vin rocked them for a few more minutes while Kerry's face dried out.

"Hey! How about if I treat you to lunch at the Haven House and we pick up food for my favorite dog?" he offered.

It was past her payday. She had not done anything about buying her usual supplies for the month.

Kerry shrugged her shoulders.

"Come on!" Vin encouraged her. "You look so great and it's almost Easter and it is a beautiful day and I want to show you off! What do you say, Kerry?"

She thought about it a little more, he guessed. He knew Kerry loved the Haven House.

"My eyes are all red. I look like hell. I have a headache. Would you go get the dog food by yourself and by the time you get back I will look and feel like a human being again?"

It made sense. The mill where they picked up food for the beast was east and the location of the restaurant would bring him back past her house again as it was west of Warmington, in yet another quaint, antique village between her house and Hebron, where she worked.

It would give her just enough time to settle down more and fix her face, which looked pretty to him no matter what color it was.

"Done!" Vin said, and he got himself off the swing and helped Kerry off since it was still moving. He wanted to tell her to put on some underwear, but it seemed risky.

Then he kissed her on her head again and watched while she walked into her house and let the dog out, and Vin went to his truck.

Notably, Luke stayed on the porch, holding a guard position between Vin and Kerry, assuming that it was this male human who had made his beloved mistress cry. He gave Vin the look he always gave Vin, which was somewhere between threat and submission to Kerry's will that he be nice to this man.

Vin was glad that the drive gave him a little time to digest what had unfolded so far that day. He had beaten Bitty in darts, only to have his triumph turn on him when Kerry thought he was wearing the stupid rabbit suit.

And his girlfriend had just propositioned the sheriff of Clifton County.

It was enough to keep Bitty and him laughing for a long time to come, and in their line of work, humor was always good.

Then he thought about Kerry again and made a mental note to buy some Easter flowers on the way back to pick her up for lunch.

But when he went inside the mill, he had a better idea.

There was a vat of baby bunnies. There was another vat of baby ducks and another of baby chicks.

Kerry loved animals. She had plenty of room, and she actually had two barns. He decided that something new to take care of and snuggle was superior to flowers. All flowers did was die.

He had a sudden vision of baby ducks frolicking in Kerry's bathtub and using it for a toilet. He had been raised with chickens and had never developed anything other than a favorite food kind of relationship with them. Besides, the beast would eat anything running around the yard as he always did, usually bringing exactly half of whatever he nabbed onto the porch and depositing it. This horrified Kerry, who spent a lot of time looking for the other halves.

Vin picked up a tiny bunny, which could be safely caged indoors, or out and was happy that way.

The thing weighed absolutely nothing. It was white with black variegated spots. It had one ear that stuck straight up and another that drooped. It had a smashed-in sort of face and the nose wiggled nonstop. It was so tiny it did not cover the palm of his hand.

"Them kind don't make for eatin'!" an ancient local in a flannel shirt advised him. Vin said nothing. He just held the tiny rabbit and looked back into the vat.

"Been sellin' a lot of those spotted ones today. I just cannot figger out what you want a rabbit fer if you can't eat the damned thing!" he continued.

Vin looked at him and smiled. The old codger was a worker in the showroom. Vin supposed he was the owner's father or something.

"Do you have any cages? And some food?" Vin asked the geezer.

"Yep! We put together a kit so's you know what to do with the damned things till they get big enough to skin," he said, and he led Vin to an area close to the register, where homemade cages held a bag of food, some wood shavings, a hanging water bottle, and a little salt spool, all for one price if a patron bought a rabbit.

"Just throw in the critter. It pretty much takes care of itself!" the codger advised.

Vin didn't care how much it all cost, but he did notice that it was about the same price as a dozen roses. And it would last longer. He paid up front and had them throw food for the beast into the back of the truck. He was so excited and happy about his gift for Kerry that he hummed all the way to her house as the little bunny sat quietly in a small box next to him on the seat.

He was happy at that moment that he had not chosen a pair of ducks.

He presented the rabbit to Kerry on her back porch, where she was waiting for him.

"Here," he said. "Happy Easter! I figure you will always know what is inside this one!"

Kerry started crying again when Vin handed her the rabbit. She held it, cooed over it, kissed it right on its little nose, and stroked it while it cuddled in the crook of her arm, and they fell in love with each other.

Her beast approached, and the tiny rabbit stuck his nose up for Luke to slurp it like a popsicle.

"Dogs always lick their food before they eat it, Kerry," Vin warned. She stroked the bunny some more.

"I'm getting a little jealous here," he said to Kerry after a few minutes. "And I'm starving. Can we secure that animal and get to lunch?"

So they set up the temporary digs on top of a table she used for crafts and such in one of her spare rooms. The door closed and actually had an outside latch so the beast could not get to the bunny. And the bunny could look out a window and get some light.

Vin told Kerry he and the boys would build a nice outdoor cage for her when the bunny got a little bigger.

When they were ready to leave, she took his hand in the doorway. She kissed him and thanked him to the point at which they usually just gave up and went to her bedroom.

But he stopped her, for some reason. He thought maybe it was so she knew he did not like her just for what went on in her bed. Or on her couch. Or in his truck. Or in her bathtub.

"Let's go to lunch!" he said. "I want to walk into Haven House with the prettiest woman in southwestern Ohio."

Especially if she wasn't wearing underwear.

Bitty came to the house one day that week when Vin told the sheriff he thought Kerry was home. He had heard, of course, how upset she had been.

Bitty told Kerry that he had been delighted with her proposal and that the last thing in the world he thought was that she was some kind of dirty woman. He told her she had made not just that day more fun for him but she had made his whole week a little better. He said he had not told a single soul about what she said to him, not even his wife, and that he never would.

She believed him.

CHAPTER 13

The day of Vin's disaster started out normally enough. He woke up at Kerry's house, pulled on his pants, and left her sleeping alone so he could run with the dog without her lagging along.

He left his gun, his wallet, and his phone in the kitchen. He opened the back door and closed it again quietly, and he and Luke set off for the fields.

Luke didn't like Vin very much unless Vin went for a walk with him. The dog knew that no matter how much they disliked each other, Vin was a good runner and would throw larger sticks farther than Kerry could and he would throw more of them.

After the walk, though, it was back to business as usual, with the beast always ready to take Vin's liver out through his nose if Kerry gave any inclination at all that the act would be appropriate.

Vin did not actually care whether or not he was loved by the dog. The dog was large and always had the same menacing look on his face, and Vin knew that the dog would probably win if anyone ever tried to harm Kerry and that no perp in his right mind would try to get into her house when the dog was there, which was all the time.

He was nice enough to the damned dog, and the thing had never tried to tear out his throat, so they settled for mutual respect.

So when Vin stepped into a fresh groundhog hole and heard a snap and saw lights flash in the darkness of near-unconsciousness from the pain of the broken bone, he was actually happy to have the dog with him, because he knew that if the dog did not come back to the house, or if it came back without Vin, Kerry might actually look for him.

He hurt so bad he couldn't do anything about the dog circling him over and over and licking his face and ears.

He wanted to call for Kerry to come and get him, but his phone was back at the house, which might as well have been a thousand miles away. He hurt so bad that shooting the foot off his leg seemed reasonable, but his gun was with his phone.

Vin did not have any idea how much time had passed when he heard Kerry's voice from someplace far away. Luke located her. The dog looked toward the house, and he looked up. Then he started barking and circling Vin.

Kerry was calling for them from the tower of her house. When she did not see Vin get up and he beckoned to her from the ground, she called 911 and said the injured party was a deputy. The dispatcher called Bitty.

Vin hurt so bad he could barely see straight, but he still cared who picked him up off the road that morning. Kerry had reached him first in her truck, but she couldn't help him up. He heard the sirens and gave her a dirty look, but she shrugged her shoulders innocently and tried not to cry.

Vin really had not figured out how he could get into the truck, so he supposed the squad would be of some help. Then the units started to appear one by one: two cruisers, an ambulance, and Bitty with Eileen in his car with him.

The funny thing was, Kerry had not thought about shutting Luke in the truck, and the dog had parked himself right next to Vin, and it didn't look like anyone was going to touch Vin without Luke's permission.

The first deputy on the scene said "Lady, get your dog!" in a mean voice, and Kerry coaxed Luke into Vin's truck. Then all she could do was stand out of the way.

They lifted Vin easily into the ambulance without much jostling of his broken ankle, but Kerry knew that for him to not protest, taking an ambulance instead of a car meant that he must have been in pain bad enough that he was trying not to scream.

Eileen stood with her, and they took Vin's truck back to the house and rode to the Warmington hospital together. Bitty rode in the ambulance with Vin.

So Kerry got a glimpse of what it was like to have an injured loved one who worked in law enforcement that day. Pretty much it meant a lot of quiet waiting and not much information or contact with the injured.

It was a full hour before she got to see Vin again. He was out of pain thanks to some pretty good IV drugs, and his foot and ankle were already casted up to his knee. He would not need surgery, but he argued with the orthopedic doctor and got him to say that he might be able to get the cast off in three weeks instead of six, if he stayed off the leg.

Bitty had him fill out papers. He told him he would send a car to take him from his apartment to and from the prescribed physical therapy appointments for the first two weeks they were necessary, which meant he could not stay with Kerry.

But since his apartment had no steps and it was a short distance from the bathroom to the three other rooms, it was probably best, she thought.

Vin handed her his two prescriptions and his wallet, and she set off to the hospital pharmacy to get them filled right away, happy to be of any help she could. It took her awhile to locate his insurance card, but she had no trouble at all finding the money.

They taught Vin how to maneuver with crutches. They told him to keep the foot elevated, and they told him how to take the pain pills.

Then Bitty drove him home after arranging for Eileen and Kerry to pick up some food for at least a couple of days, food Vin could easily fix for himself. They also picked up takeout for lunch.

They went to the grocery store together, and Kerry paid for everything with the credit card she had seen Vin use almost exclusively. She felt very powerful in control of his wallet, she related to Eileen. She also said she had not seen pictures of any other women while looking for his cards.

"That's a universal sign we are women!" Bitty's wife laughed.

"Always locate the money, count the credit cards, and look for the pictures of the other women!"

CHAPTER 14

Vin wasn't a good patient because he did not like to be helpless. He didn't like everybody fawning over him, he didn't like having to work so hard to get to the bathroom, he didn't like the boys staying with him at night and having to help him shower, he didn't like having to eat whatever was stuffed into his refrigerator by Eileen, Joan, and Kerry, and he didn't like not working.

Bitty arranged for him to proofread reports hastily handwritten by deputies in the field, and Vin was actually pretty good at it, but when the guys started calling him the Spell-Check Nazi, he gave up.

Kerry told him he was grumpy. He didn't like that, either. But then she demonstrated that not all his parts were injured and that he did not have to be mobile to be intimate with her, and he felt a little better about being stuck in one place.

She said something about his ex-wife visiting him and bringing him what he said were his favorite foods. When he went to the fridge after that remark, he found all of Joan's blue-lidded containers shoved toward the back of the refrigerator and Kerry's red-lidded containers prominently displayed in the front.

So he told her that he and Joan had shared nearly twenty pretty good years and made two boys together, and if they could occupy the same planet without killing each other, it was all good. He said that Joan was nice enough to bring the boys over every night and pick them up for school and that she was just trying to help their father.

But Kerry remained in a snit about it until Vin's temporary cast was replaced with a walking cast and he could stay with her at her house again.

While Vin was incapacitated, Kerry drove him to a place that sold manufactured homes. She took him to another that sold log cabins. They had to ride in his truck because he had to stretch out, and he told Bitty that the worst part of the whole broken-bone thing was sitting in the back seat of his own truck while his girlfriend drove it.

He had spoken to her about possibly building something small on some land someday, and she said she wanted to show him some of the nontraditional options.

He supposed she already guessed that if ever they decided to make their relationship a forever one, Vin was not going to live in her crazy house.

And he had long ago asked if she planned to stay in her house forever, and she had said that she didn't see how that would be possible, that she was just sort of hanging on to it because she loved it so much.

So Vin's head filled with possibilities again. He and Bitty had walked about a hundred miles over beautiful, available acreage. Vin definitely was tired as hell of living in his apartment. With Kerry, he had seen small houses that were not only efficient but they also were nice to look at and affordable, but he had two boys who would be going to college.

Then again, he sure loved the log cabins. So he used his time off waiting for the damned ankle to fully mend to call and ask about things like digging a well, a septic system, and having electricity furnished on unimproved county property.

He made a file on his computer with all the information and kept a desk drawer full of all of the paperwork.

In July, Kerry called him one day on her lunch break and told him that a lady had come to the pharmacy who was recently widowed. She said she and her husband had planned to build their dream home on some land just inside of Clifton but now that would never happen. She said she was going to move to Florida.

Kerry gave Vin the approximate location of the lady's acreage, and ten days later, Vin owned his ten acres of Clifton County.

By the end of August, the widow's huge motor home was parked on a new concrete pad with a gravel driveway on the land, and Vin left his apartment and moved into it.

Vin and his dad and the boys spent a hot summer weekend assembling and painting a new shed, a concrete block firepit was dug and surrounded by a wall of stone, and a propane grill was bought and tested.

Except for the rocking and rolling when the summer squalls popped up, Vin just loved the place and said he had never felt such peace.

Footers were dug, the first step in building a roofed carport of sorts, which would protect the motor home from the weight and damage of ice and snow. And that would keep the hottest of the summer sunrays off its top. It was going to be wide enough to accommodate his truck next to the home, and over time, Vin planned to have it enclosed, and at that point it would make a great garage.

CHAPTER 15

The first party at Vin's new place was a surprise for his birthday that year.

He had absolutely no idea about the party. He rushed home from work that afternoon expecting to change his clothes and meet Kerry in town for a quiet dinner, and instead he found his boys, Kerry, her beast, her daughter, his dad, and the Bitterns, all of them.

There was a pop-up canopy, a couple of portable tables decked out in birthday paper, a bunch of lawn chairs, burgers already on the grill, a couple of coolers, and four or five covered dishes, which Vin knew contained his favorite picnic foods. There was a homemade cake under a large glass dome, and his name was on it.

Kerry made a point of saying that no one had a key to his motor home, so they all had to wait for him outside.

She had one, of course. And Vin had a key to her place, though she never locked the damned door. But she wisely did not display to any of the birthday guests that she and Vin were at such a point in their relationship, albeit a minor one for them.

His boys, her daughter, and his dad did not need to know anything, and it was of no concern to the Bitterns.

He winked at her when she denied owning a key so she knew she had made the right move.

When he opened the door, all eleven people entered and toured his new home. It was a tight fit. They quickly exited so he could change his clothes, and then the party began.

Kerry had brought party hats and necklaces and those irritating blower things, and Vin noted that no one seemed to enjoy those childish implements more than adults.

Something else Vin noted was that Luke loved absolutely everyone except for him.

The dinner was delicious, and when they cut into the cake, it was a checkered cake, alternating blocks of chocolate and vanilla, and no one guessed how Kerry had made it so. She never did describe the process.

His dad bought him a brand-new lawn mower, which fit perfectly in the shed along with the grill, and the boys had their first driving experiences with it. Bitty's gift was a lock for the door of the shed, and he brought the tools to install it.

Vin's dad and the boys attached the lock to the shed door while Bitty cooked burgers and hot dogs. Kerry and Eileen set out the rest of the spread, and all Vin had to do was sit there and watch and enjoy.

They would not let him do anything else.

As the evening went on, they built a fire in his new firepit, and Vin confirmed to himself that his recent move was exactly what he needed, and so was the pretty woman who sat just close enough to him and looked lovingly at him just enough that he felt even luckier.

All in all, Vin decided, it had not been such a bad thing to turn another year older. And that night when he followed Kerry home with all her stuff and her dog and spent much of the night with her, he didn't feel any older at all. She wore out long before he did.

CHAPTER 16

That summer, the corn in the fields surrounding Kerry's house and yard grew to over seven feet tall. The towering stalks and leaves were a beautiful mix of greens, and the sound of the rows of plants, hundreds of thousands of them softly rustling and pollenating themselves in the summer breezes, was very calming. The light, pleasant scent of sun-warmed cornstalks was always there.

The beast liked nothing more than running through the rows of corn. Kerry said he spent hours in the fields, trotting up and down the rows, and she thought he might be looking for mice or toads. She spotted him from her tower window when he was missing. His favorite trick was to flush out small herds of deer while Kerry and Vin walked or Kerry walked alone, and he always aimed the frantically high-bounding creatures right at them.

It was alarming as hell.

Kerry and Vin spent that first summer together spending days off at the lake with the boys and sometimes including Elizabeth, waterskiing and swimming and cooking out at Kerry's place or his at the end of the day.

He and the boys helped out at his dad's whenever they could, and Vin made certain the boys mowed his father's acreage and Kerry's too. He taught them how to drive his father's tractor and how to perform the constant maintenance necessary to keep the thing running.

Vin took the boys camping in his motor home. They agreed that it was luxury living compared to tent camping. They went to

Kentucky to one of the massive lakes there and fished and swam and talked a lot. They didn't shower for four days, and they only ate when they were hungry. They played poker at night and used peanuts for chips. They wrestled on the floor and on the grass.

Most important of all was that they talked and talked and talked.

Vin and Joan had agreed upon nearly all things having to do with parenting, and that did not change after the divorce. They both agreed that as the boys grew into young men, it was better to tell them how they personally felt about dating, sex, drugs, friends, God, work, and school as opposed to just telling the boys what they were not allowed to do.

This method gave the boys a sounding board with the voice of experience, and most of the time it worked. They were normal kids who at times tried the limits and made some bad decisions, but thanks to Vin, they always paid some price.

Most of all, they knew not to cross Vin's boundaries of acceptable behavior because the consequences were never worth it.

If one of them got into a fight at school, Vin signed up for the following weekend at Bitty's jail and took that boy along for the experience. After a day of listening to the crude remarks and observing the cruder behavior of the inmates and after having to mop urine off the floors and serve the meals through slots in the cells, a lesson was learned.

After having to eat with the prisoners in the cafeteria and understanding that it would be easy enough to end up a resident there, the lesson was solidified.

When Vin dropped one or the other boy off at a local run-down farm after prearranging with the farmer to find the worst chores possible for that son for an entire day, he didn't have to say a word when he picked the exhausted boy up at the end of that day and dropped him back at Joan's.

And all he had to do was escort one of them into the juvenile detention center and hang around for an hour or so and take a tour, and whatever that son had done to cause himself trouble was rarely repeated.

Vin thought it must be tough to have him for a father. He liked it that way.

So talking was always good. What was missing after the divorce was the evening meal with the boys and two parents at the table, talking about the day's events and making plans for the future.

What was missing after the divorce was Vin's final check of the house and a look in on the boys before he went to bed with Joan every night for nearly twenty years, and the satisfaction that everything was all right.

Those regrets would never go away, he knew, but his new relationship with Kerry and his ability to spend as much time as possible with the boys softened the raw edges somewhat.

CHAPTER 17

A couple of times a month, Vin took Kerry to a nice restaurant and a movie for a more formal kind of date. He did not want her to think she always had to cook for him or that she was not worth spending money on. Plus he loved the look on both the men's and the women's faces when he walked across a restaurant floor escorting Kerry and demonstrated that they were together by lightly holding her elbow or placing his hand upon the small of her back. Kerry was the kind of pretty that made people stop and take a look.

Vin was not possessive or controlling, which was a good thing because no one could possess or control Kerry. But he loved the exclusive nature of their relationship, the casual but respectful way they treated each other knowing that there was no one else for either one of them. There was a difference in that and taking each other for granted, Vin knew, and he did not want Kerry to ever think she was not special to him.

As summer came to a close, the local towns and villages prepared for the autumn harvest and festival season, and Vin took his turn manning the county sheriff booth at the Clifton County Fair. Of particular interest to the fairgoers were the canine deputies.

Bitty had six of the amazing dogs working for the county. They were various purebreds, and two were mutts. All were crazy intelligent, and Bitty often pointed out to his deputies that these dogs worked just as hard as their human counterparts did and all they asked for in return was a tennis ball or a treat.

One year when the county was particularly hard up for money to give raises to his staff, Bitty brought in one of the K9 handlers and his dog. He read a report detailing how the dog had been accurate at a 95 percent rate since the department acquired him. He said the dog was due for a raise and displayed a jar of dog treats on his podium and told the deputies to think about it.

Late in August, Vin and Kerry each had three days off during the week, so they took his motor home north to Lake Erie and did all the local things before the last summer holiday brought crowds to the area for one final summer party.

Kerry's daughter stayed at the house to watch the dog and the bunny, which Kerry had named Clover. Elizabeth brought three friends down from college with her, and when Vin opened Kerry's refrigerator on a hunch just before he and Kerry departed, he was not surprised to find that it was completely full of cans of beer. He immediately called the four girls into the kitchen, opened the frig door to display the cause of his concern, and gave them a brief but sobering lecture on underage beer drinking.

He told them he had already asked deputies to check on them night and day, and he told them they needed to think about their actions and that he had better not get a call while he was away. Then he told them to have fun.

When he and Kerry drove the motor home out of her long driveway, she was glaring at Vin, and she did not speak to him until they had left the county. But he already knew that she had bought the beer for the girls and that she could not say a word.

After a relaxing and scenic three-hour drive, Vin parked his motor home where he had made a reservation, and they balanced it and hooked it up for camping together for the first time. Then they set off to tour the islands on the lake.

They rented bicycles and rode them around the largest island. They took a ferryboat to a winery and drank too much. They ate junk food and drank local beer in tiny bars along a boardwalk, and they climbed to the top of a lighthouse and enjoyed the view of the part of the Lake Erie where Admiral Samuel Hazard Perry had defeated the British during the War of 1812.

They went swimming in the huge lake at an actual beach with lots of sand, and they swam at night in the pool at the RV camp.

Kerry had warned Vin not to ever get her into a hot tub after dark, and late one of the nights he found out why. He just hoped no one saw them.

On that trip, at the top of the lighthouse, Vin told Kerry he was in love with her. Without any hesitation at all, she told him she was in love with him too. All in all, that was quite a trip.

CHAPTER 18

Vin did not tell Kerry about his football tickets until he was certain she had a couple of weekends off during the season.

Then he surprised her. She was not easy to do anything wonderful for because she was very sensitive to seeming dependent. She did not want to be supported by a man she slept with, she said, because that would make her a promiscuous whore.

Vin had attempted to talk her out of that belief a couple of times, but he gave up. He told her that when people were in love, they just needed to do whatever they wanted to do for each other, but she said she could not do much for him, so she didn't want him to spend money on her unless it was for both of them.

The football tickets were for both of them.

He told her the night before the first game. She thought they were going to a flea market in the morning and looking at cabins in the afternoon.

She was so excited she could barely sleep, and he knew because he attempted to sleep next to her. Finally he thought of a way to exhaust her without leaving her bed, and it worked out well for him, too.

They decided to take her car for the ride because it took up the least amount of parking space, which was at a premium in Columbus on game days.

They made arrangements to meet her daughter and a friend or two after the game for dinner, ate breakfast, fed the bunny, walked the dog, and were off.

The first blowout was not that big a deal. The second one was a real problem, however, because then they were out of spare tires.

They had to be towed to a tire store, and Vin did not hesitate to buy four new tires, ignoring Kerry's argument that she still had two good ones, which she didn't. Fortunately the tire guy spoke over Vin and told her that she was in danger of blowing those two tires on the way home.

The tire place changed the oil while they installed the tires and filled the fluids, checked the brakes, etc., so although Vin was out a few hundred bucks, he would feel good about Kerry's car for a few months and she had good tires for winter.

Kerry thanked Vin, but she was embarrassed.

She said, "That tire guy probably thinks I am one of those women who get things from men in return for sex."

At least she did not say the words promiscuous whore, thought Vin.

"I told him you were my wife," Vin lied. That changed everything. Kerry was all right with that. In fact, she seemed to like the idea.

The game was great. The band was great. It was preseason, but the atmosphere and the fun of the whole experience was regular season. Kerry was fun and pretty, asked for nothing, and actually paid attention to the game.

And for the first time, Vin started to think about what their lives would be like if she was his wife.

He stopped thinking about it when he remembered that she was never going to let go of her house and he was never going to have anything to do with that place.

After the game, he treated Kerry, Elizabeth, and three of her friends to dinner. When they left the restaurant, Elizabeth asked Kerry to buy the girls a twelve-pack of beer, and Vin said no.

Kerry said she was paying for it, and Elizabeth did not really know what to do about this man controlling her plans and her mother, but Vin was adamant.

He knew what to say without embarrassing Elizabeth in front of her friends. He made it all his fault because of his job. He didn't let Kerry say a word, and he gave the girls money to buy snacks and other beverages for their after-game party.

He already knew they would buy beer from another source, but the person who got it for them was not going to be him. Or Kerry.

He did the refusal, the alternate option, and the goodbyes so quickly there was no argument or appearance of anger, and then he got Kerry to the car and shut her door before she could explode on him.

She didn't explode. She just sat in silence and pouted. It was a good forty-five minutes before they were on the highway for the return to Clifton County, and she did not speak to him the entire time.

Then all she said was, "I wish you could let go of being a deputy sometimes."

Fair enough. Vin wished he could let go of being a deputy sometimes, too. And Kerry never tried to pay him back for the auto maintenance, so it was all good.

They looked at the calendar when they got back to her house and made a plan to go to more games together.

CHAPTER 19

Vin and his sons helped out on his father's farm a few days at the end of that summer. It was hot, sweaty work, but no matter how far farming technology had come, some of the work had to be done manually and repeatedly over the hundred or so acres, and Vin's father was happy to have the help.

Kerry brought over dinner a couple of the evenings when she got off work, and she said she had never seen anyone eat as much as the four Fackler men.

She left cakes and cookies for them when she went home, alone, and Vin told her that, pretty much, she was an angel. She scoffed and grumbled that a man would say anything on a full stomach. Vin thought she was probably right.

Summer in Clifton County turned to fall with the subtle changes of the landscape and then arrival of sunset dramatically earlier each night.

The annual run of the Medieval Festival, located between Kerry's house and the lake, went into full swing in early September, and three times the department had to clear campers from Kerry's back fields.

These were itinerant carnival workers who traveled all over the country and set up and took down booths, rides, and games over and over again and made decent money doing their work, but it was seasonal labor. As fall approached, they had to think about where they were going to get money for the winter, so a very small percentage of them turned to theft. There was always an increase in breaking and entering complaints while the festival was in Clifton County, and calls for cars in the parking lot that had their contents removed while the owners were having fun at the fair were common.

Over one hundred of them came to Clifton County annually for the entire two months of the Medieval Festival, and except for the illegal camping and the marijuana smoking and the overuse of alcohol and the fights, they were a peaceful bunch, Vin thought.

But some of them brought with them increasing suspicion of being part of the general drug trade, and their oft-suspected acquisition and sale of substances to the locals was of some concern to the department.

So when the festival was in full swing and Kerry told Vin one evening that she thought there was something funny going on in the fields behind her house, he acted like he would watch for signs, but he knew Kerry already was doing that.

There was a small airfield about three miles from Kerry's place, on a long road that transversed several counties, and this airport served the crop dusters and hot-air ballooners and several of the wealthier farmers who owned private planes and sheltered them there. This road ran parallel to Kerry's place, and the generally used flight path was perpendicular to that road, so planes began their approach to it just about over Kerry's place, using her tall landmark house as their marker as they crossed the state route she lived on.

The airport was only manned during daylight hours, but one landing strip was illuminated at night just enough that an emergency or night landing could be safely made there.

If the county helicopter needed to be put into action, it was no problem as there was no locked gate or restricted access to the entire airport. If a plane flew into or out of the airport during the night, no one took notice because the office and tower were not staffed between sundown and sunup. No logs were kept of the evening flights in or out. No radio traffic was necessary.

Kerry explained her suspicion to Vin one morning over breakfast. She said that sometimes in the wee hours of the night, planes flew at a low altitude over her place, with the engines cut just before they reached her house from the road.

If she was awake, she said, she heard them approach and then heard the swoosh as they flew over her house. She said if she moved quickly enough, she could run to the back window of her second story and see the red and green port and starboard running lights dip down over the cornfield and then suddenly shoot upward again as the engine was restarted and the plane resumed altitude and headed in a straight line toward the airport.

She claimed that just at that point, as the planes began to gain altitude again, a pickup truck with no lights on sped down her lane and went toward the area where the plane had been. She said that after a few more minutes, the truck left again, driving right past her house at a high rate of speed, and it was this part that alarmed her.

She said that hunters and farmers often went down her lane in the darkness, but they always had their headlights on, and pretty much she knew who they were and what they were doing.

Vin was actually alarmed by what Kerry told him, but he knew that if he acted more interested than he was, Kerry would try to do something on her own to answer her own questions.

She didn't like to ask for help, and she wasn't asking for help. She just wanted his professional opinion, but not his advice.

His advice was to let his department handle it. He told Kerry to call. It was a simple and direct more-than-a-request, and she knew he meant it as an order but that he dare not make a big deal of it.

He went to the window at the end of one of the two upstairs hallways where she had said she could see the incoming planes at night, and sure enough, she had a chair and binoculars, a camera, and a heavy-duty flashlight there at the ready. When he saw them and turned his gaze back to the doorway, where Kerry was standing and fidgeting with her hands, trying to look innocent, he hoped his look gave her all the warning she needed, and he again repeated that she was to make a call.

He told her to lock her damned doors, but he knew it was a worthless order. Kerry had once told him, when asked, why she never remarried after her divorce when Elizabeth was only a toddler, and she had thrown her head back and said, "I don't like men telling me what to do."

In reality, Vin was not that concerned for Kerry's safety, as drug dealers usually left the bystanders alone unless they tried to interfere. Operating with neighboring folks unaware and unsuspecting was a perfect setting for their evil craft. People who saw nothing and feared nothing could report nothing. The corn didn't talk.

Nevertheless, he spoke with Bitty, and his route was changed to the southwestern portion of Clifton County, which meant Kerry and her crazy house were part of his normal routine. He didn't tell her, knowing that when she decided to call and report things, he would be the likely respondent if he were on duty and she would have nothing to say about it.

And he could legally watch over the property and she could not do anything about that, either.

Then one particularly pleasant night when he was staying with Kerry and she had the windows open all over the place, all twenty-something of them, she awakened in the middle of the night and jumped out of bed, and the dog made a loud yawning sound and followed her out of the room.

Vin got up and followed them to the end of the hall, where Kerry motioned him to come to the window.

Sure enough, what she had described unfolded right in front of them both. When a small truck sped past the house, Vin told Kerry to stay put, and he ran outside to catch a plate number, undetected, he hoped.

He was crouched next to one of her barns as the truck returned, but in the darkness he could not get a color or make/model of the truck, and of course the plates were not illuminated.

When he turned back toward the house, he literally ran into Kerry, who had followed him outside. He almost had a heart attack, and when he yelled at her, she would not speak to him or sleep with him the rest of the night.

He spoke with Bitty again, and they made a loose plan to begin an investigation. He didn't tell Kerry.

So when she ran into the darkness while he wasn't there a few nights later and very excitedly called him and reported that the truck was a red Chevy, information she garnered by shining a flashlight on the exiting vehicle, Vin was not surprised. He was just furious. He knew she had gone outside, as the angle of the window and the distance to the speeding truck would have made it impossible to get that information from the house. She could not have seen the color of the truck without shining the light on it, and she might have been spotted by the driver.

Now Vin was upset, but not as much as Kerry when he told her she might be in hot water. Bitty spoke to her in person himself, with Vin in uniform next to him. Vin had complained that all he could do was make suggestions. Bitty could lay down the law, and of course he called his friend a wimp.

"You can't put a saddle on a hummingbird," Vin told him.

Bitty's face-to-face message was clear: let the department handle this.

But they couldn't handle it fast enough for Kerry.

She did some things like putting up more "No Trespassing" and "Private Drive" signs. She did start to lock her doors. She measured the entrance to her property for a gate, but when she priced it, the cost was prohibitive.

The singular damning thing she did was to hammer long nails into pieces of scrap wood and arrange them onto the lane at night so that anyone entering the back of her acreage would not be able to proceed. When she heard the commotion, she planned to call for help, and she felt that at least the department would have the truck, if not the driver.

She caught another deputy making a routine drive down the lane as he had been ordered to do. Not one but two of his tires blew out, and when he exited his vehicle and saw what had occurred, he went right to the house.

He wasn't very nice to the lone occupant, and he did not know she had a connection of sorts to the department. He was writing out the second of three tickets he intended to issue when the tow truck and a second cruiser sent to pick him up came to the scene, and the driver of the second cruiser was Vin.

Bitty made another appearance, and this time, Kerry went out of the crime prevention business. She even baked plates of apology cookies for the deputy who had his tires flattened, for Bitty, and a plate for Vin.

Smart woman that Vin knew she was, none of the three was mad at Kerry after that.

Vin never knew what Bitty said to Kerry that second meeting, but whatever, it worked.

On a hunch, Vin had Bitty order a helicopter to fly over the fields behind Kerry's house by daylight. The report came back: three square-shaped areas in the cornfields where the corn had been knocked down from above, like something heavy was dropped from an airplane.

Something like large, heavy packages of drugs. They brought in a canine unit, and there was a positive result, likely from some residue that escaped when the loads hit the ground.

A broad search of the living areas of the Medieval Fair folks with the dog told them that most of the people who worked there smoked pot but did not reveal any significant quantity of illegal substances.

The investigations widened. Vin drove around the employee area of the Medieval Festival and saw a lot of older small dark-colored pickup trucks, including several red ones, and scanned all the plates.

The results displayed evidence that more than one of them had at least once been involved in stops, which resulted in drug arrests, albeit nothing large.

Bitty felt it would be too much of a coincidence if the festival folks were not involved with whatever was going on at Kerry's, because it was just too convenient. The activity had probably been going on for years, but no one had occupied the house much of the past fifty or so of its one hundred thirty years of existence until Kerry moved in.

To stake out the area night after night would be a waste of time and personnel, Bitty had decided, and Vin agreed. Plus an overflying plane would see the cruiser roofs if they were in the fields or on Kerry's road.

So Vin volunteered to stay at the residence every night.

"Big of you!" Bitty responded.

"That's what she said!" Vin replied.

CHAPTER 20

The night everything happened was about as hot and muggy as a September night in Ohio can get. Kerry had all the windows closed and the air conditioners on, and fans were running on high to circulate the air-conditioned air.

They watched the late news that night, and Kerry fell asleep on the couch, the beast at her feet.

Vin woke her up to come upstairs to bed, and she promised to be right up. He fell asleep before she got there, and Kerry fell asleep again right where she was on the couch.

At about three in the morning, Luke went crazy. He barked and howled, and Kerry thought he smelled or heard a coyote close to Clover's outdoor cage, so she opened the door and let him out, just as Vin shouted for her to keep the door closed. He heard a noise and instinctively knew someone was outside the house. The dog had sounded different, too. He sounded like the canine units when they wanted to get loose for a pursuit of a suspect.

But Kerry did not hear him until Luke was outside, so she went out to retrieve him. As she neared her barns, she saw a truck headed for the back acreage, right where Luke had headed.

One call from Vin, and full squad was on the way.

Vin pulled on his pants, shoes, T-shirt, and holstered weapon. He ran to the back window for Kerry's big flashlight and opened the window and called for her and got no answer.

There was no moon, and he couldn't see anything at all as he exited the house to contact the first cruiser, but mostly he needed to get Kerry and her dog back to the house. She needed to be inside, and the dog needed to be out of the way if the professional dogs were dispatched so as to avoid confusion.

Vin went to his truck and retrieved his vest and badge and intercepted the first cruiser on the scene. They headed past both barns and down the road behind the house, where there was no sign of Kerry and no sign of the beast, so Vin exited the cruiser and started to call her.

He saw the canine unit drive past and heard the helicopter in the distance and saw the red and blue flashes of more cruisers on the road in front of the house for traffic control and to halt any vehicle attempting to exit the property.

But he couldn't find Kerry. He ran into the corn and called in all directions. He was slapped in the face by about a million corn leaves, and the hairy dust on them filled his nose and eyes.

Then he heard her scream. She was behind him, nearer to the house, away from all the help.

Vin cursed and drew his gun then headed for the scream. The copter flew over him. He heard the bullhorns. He heard a scream again, an agonized, gurgling sound, and his blood ran cold, but he knew he was getting closer. Behind him, he heard a deputy calling his name, and he responded, shouting that he was east of the house traveling west.

And then, in the blue light of the flashlight, he saw Kerry.

"Oh god!" he gasped.

She was wearing a long white cotton nightgown, only in the light it was mostly red. She was barefoot, standing over her dog. She was covered with either her own or the dog's blood. She was sobbing hysterically, but someone crying that hard, Vin knew, was probably not hurt very badly because she had her throat and both of her lungs and she was conscious.

Vin pushed his way through the last rows of corn and got to her as she sank down onto the ground over her dog.

The body of her dog.

A quick assessment demonstrated that the dog had been stabbed multiple times. The blood had apparently been spurting and flowing when Kerry arrived, drenching her, but now it was just glistening on Luke's coat, a sign that his heart had stopped. Vin shone his light in Luke's open eyes, and there was no reaction. Luke's mouth was open, and his flaccid tongue was blue. He helped Kerry to her feet, but she could barely stand up because her feet were all cut up from running on the gravel road and through the dry cornfield. Vin still did not know if she had been hurt by whomever stabbed the dog.

There was nothing to do but get Kerry out of there. Whomever had done this to her dog was still in the area. He could have been three feet away and been invisible, hidden by the dense corn and the darkness.

The other deputy reached them, and Vin told him to call for an ambulance and pursue the suspect.

Then he picked Kerry up to piggyback her toward her house. She didn't want to leave her dog.

She cried and tried to cling to the dog, but Vin slid her hands off Luke's coat and managed to pull her away.

"I don't want to leave him!" she shouted to Vin, who said quietly and sadly, "Kerry, there is nothing you can do for him now."

Then she just continued to cry. Vin hoped her feet were not actively bleeding, but he could not see anything, so he just kept going toward the safety of the house as she clung to his shoulders and sobbed. Her head was down, so Vin took the brunt of the battering of the cornstalks and the blizzard of dust.

He had an odd thought: soybeans instead of corn would have eliminated this entire scenario.

Another cruiser came toward them as Vin reached the road. The deputy driving it helped load Kerry into the cruiser, and then Vin switched course and had him drive back to where the others were and where the ambulance had gone when it passed them on the road as it turned left toward the woods.

Kerry would be safer there, and the medics could see to her, he knew. Plus he wanted to be part of taking down the son of a bitch who killed her dog and was probably headed toward the house to kill her when her dog intercepted him and paid for it with his life.

For all he knew at that moment, there could be more than one suspect in the field, but now the canine deputy could make quick work of any or all of them. The helicopter was hovering, so it was possible a visual ID had been made.

The once total darkness was now illuminated with several lights.

The canine handler called for backup, and Vin left Kerry with the group and went back into the corn to assist him.

Sure enough, about an acre due west, there was the deputy, a very happy, snarling canine deputy, and a very unhappy suspect cowering on the ground and begging to have the dog called back. He was covered with blood, which could not have been from the precise puncture wounds of the K9's teeth in his leg.

Vin picked him up.

"Where did all this blood come from?" he demanded.

"The dog bit me!" the smelly whiny man cried. Vin shook him.

"Which dog…this one or the one you stabbed to death?"

"Both of them! Please get that monster away from me!" he whined.

Vin punched him in the gut.

"You didn't see that!" he said under his breath to the other deputy. And the dog said nothing.

The handler restrained the canine, and Vin cuffed the suspect and help came to drag him back to a cruiser for a trip to Bitty's jail.

There was a second suspect, also apprehended by the deputies. He had been in possession of a gun. And in the back of the truck was about fifty pounds of assorted controlled substances bundled like gifts from Santa Claus, which would never make it to the streets.

There was Kerry, seated on the tailgate of the ambulance, having her feet cleaned up and bandaged. Vin approached, and the paramedic told him that her feet were all chewed up but that she did not need stitches. She needed a tetanus shot.

"Vin," said Kerry through still-flowing tears, "I need to get my Luke. I can't just leave him in the corn all night!"

Fortunately, the sheriff appeared at the scene just in time.

"We need the dog for evidence, Kerry," Bitty said with authority. "We'll talk about what to do with him when we are finished."

Then he gathered the deputies and started to sort things out.

Vin took Kerry back to the house in a cruiser. He sat her on her kitchen counter near the sink, and they started to clean her up after he scrubbed the blood off his own hands and arms. He fetched her another gown, and between the two of them, she looked fairly presentable when Bitty joined them after a while.

He checked on Kerry and told her it looked like she would be all right, and then he said he needed to speak with Vin in private, so they went outside onto the porch, where Vin heard the wild news.

Bitty spoke to Vin in a low voice so Kerry would not hear, but what he said almost caused Vin to shout in disbelief: the beast, Luke, was still alive.

During the cleanup, when the deputies were gathering evidence, the medics were asked to retrieve the big dog with a stretcher, and when they came out of the woods, they were in a rush. They said the dog was still breathing.

Some fresh deputies who had come at the change of shift thought Luke was a canine unit and instructed that he be taken to the local emergency room, the human one, by the ambulance.

Bitty had actually left the premises, but when he heard that a canine unit was being transported, he returned. The dog was en route to the hospital by then, but he straightened out the confusion when he spoke to the actual canine handler, who had his perfectly satisfied and healthy dog with him and had left the scene. So he drove to the hospital in Warmington.

He did not call ahead to tell them to stop treating the dog.

Even Bitty thought the dog deserved a chance after what he had done that night.

When the sheriff got to the hospital, the emergency room professionals were working on Kerry's dog, and they said they were making some progress.

They said the dog had one deep wound and several superficial ones and had lost a lot of blood. Bitty did not have the heart to tell them to stop, but he did arrange for the dog to be taken to the department veterinarian as soon as it was possible. He was speaking to Vin to inform him that after the dog left the hospital, someone other than the Clifton County Sheriff Department was going to have to bear the financial responsibility for the dog's medical care.

"So my question to you is, do you want the vet to keep trying?"

"Sure," Vin said without hesitation, asking himself, what else was he supposed to do?

"I knew you loved that dog," Bitty said, and then he left for the night after checking on Kerry once more.

Kerry was doing a little better. She seemed to have resigned herself to the fact that her dog was gone, but her feet were beginning to swell and hurt.

Between the porch and the house, Vin had decided not to tell her about the miracle, because if it went the other way, she would have lost the dog twice.

Vin carried her upstairs to her bed, got her some pain tablets and some water, and checked the bandages for fresh blood. There was none, so the cuts had ceased to bleed at least.

He jumped into her shower, rinsing off the sweat, the dog blood, the perp's foul stench, and about a million little feathery itchy things that had covered the corn leaves and now covered him. He had some old clothes there from doing yard work, so he tossed his bloody clothes into the laundry pile from the night and put on the clean ones.

Then he turned out the lights and lay down next to Kerry and waited for the phone to ring.

He tried to get some rest, but with that kind of event just winding down, adrenaline was still keeping his eyes open and his muscles twitching.

He went back downstairs and threw his clothes and Kerry's bloody things into her washer and cleaned up the kitchen from the earlier mess they had made.

Kerry just slept. Which was great because it meant she wasn't afraid of anything anymore. She was just exhausted.

CHAPTER 21

Just before dawn, Vin took another call, this time from the vet. Vin walked down a hallway with the phone and entered another room and closed the door.

"This is Deputy Fackler," he said quietly.

It was the vet, the one who took care of the canine units. She reported that Luke was in stable condition and was still receiving transfusions kept on hand for the canine units, but that it was too early to determine if there was any brain damage from loss of blood and therefore loss of oxygen to his brain.

How in the hell would anyone know if that damned dog had brain damage or not? Vin wanted to ask her.

Then she gave him an estimate of the costs of the care up to that point, and Vin was speechless.

She asked if she should continue.

"Yes. And thank you. Keep me updated."

He whistled through his teeth as soon as he disconnected.

There went the cover to his motor home, he thought.

It wasn't even seven o'clock in the morning when the reporters showed up and the television camera crews parked all over Kerry's lawn.

Her feet were so sore she was shivering as she stirred in the early light. Vin helped her to the bathroom, and she took some pain tablets, then he gathered the clean clothes she requested and told her to call him when she was dressed.

He phoned Bitty, and the sheriff said he was on his way.

"Bless you!" Vin told him, not wanting to speak to even one reporter about anything at all.

But Bitty would see this as a wonderful opportunity to highlight the great work of the Clifton County deputies. Bitty was born for this kind of crap, and it was one of the few things that were dissimilar about him and Vin as they were growing up together.

Vin had always let Bitty do the talking, and he was grateful today to let him continue the tradition.

Vin went outside, greeted the dozen or so reporters, and had them assemble near the front porch so Bitty would have a stage upon which to hand out his bullshit. One of the TV guys knew him as law.

The reporters wanted to know why he was still at the house, and he said, "I am a friend of the resident. I am here in an unofficial capacity." He said it in such a way that they let him alone.

Bitty came with a huge box of donuts for the reporters and took over just as Vin got another call from the vet.

The damned dog was doing exceptionally well, walking, drinking water, and urinating, and even though he had sutures and drains, they wanted to release him at about noon, she said.

No matter what, Vin decided, being able to tell the pretty woman inside the house, the one who couldn't walk and who almost got killed the night before, that her beloved, stupid dog was coming home after some kind of Lazarus deal was going to be worth it.

Vin told Bitty the news about the dog without Kerry knowing it. Bitty excused himself and went into public servant mode on the front porch. Vin went to check on Kerry.

Then just as Kerry started to get weepy about losing her dog despite the satisfaction that two hard-ass criminals were apprehended on her property and put out of business, Vin decided to tell her about Luke.

Even more worth it was the fact that Kerry was naked in a bubble bath, with her bandaged feet hung over the edge so as not to get wet.

Kerry was ecstatic. The pain had subsided. She was comfortable and clean and well. What was a guy supposed to do with that? Especially with his boss just downstairs on the porch.

They made it silent and quick, with a minimal splash of water onto the floor.

They dressed and sat on the back porch and waited for Bitty, who just could not stop smiling. He had even saved a few donuts, which they enjoyed over coffee in the kitchen.

Vin knew he would hear about his ability to brew and serve coffee without asking Kerry where anything was when he and Bitty were alone somewhere, sometime.

As Bitty left, he suggested Vin take Kerry to Urgent Care to get her feet looked at and rebandaged. It was a great idea. Kerry stood for eight hours a day when she worked, and she was not going to be able to do that until she could walk again.

The nurse practitioner at Urgent Care was an old friend of Vin's from when he was married to Joan. Linda's husband, Rich, was a Warmington firefighter.

Linda cleaned, dressed, and rebandaged Kerry's feet expertly; gave her a tetanus shot and a prescription for better pain control. She showed Vin the feet and showed them to Kerry with a mirror.

Kerry's feet looked as if she had walked over broken glass for about a mile and then a professional baseball player had used them for batting practice. But her pedicure was still perfect.

Vin got the prescription for her and gave her some water so she could take the medication and start feeling better, and they went to get the dog.

The reunion between Kerry and her beast was very touching. The damned dog was shaved over about one-third of his body. He had dozens of stitches and a couple of tubes sticking out of him, and he could barely walk at all, but he made it across the small room to Kerry, who sat on the floor to greet him because she could barely walk as well.

Luke had one of those plastic halo cones around his neck, and Vin said he looked like a martini.

But actually, he did believe that this mutt had saved Kerry from serious injury or even from being stabbed to death just the night before, and for that, he would always be grateful. There was a bag full of medications and a packet of instructions for his care.

So Vin got his lame girl and her lame dog into the truck and went back inside and set up payment arrangements and thanked everyone for the care.

He picked up lunch at a drive-through and took Kerry and the dog home. He had to walk the damned thing and practically had to hold him up so Luke could relieve himself, and then he had to help Kerry to the bathroom, too.

All three of them slept the afternoon away in Kerry's TV room, and all three of them slept for a long, long time.

The boys called him late in the afternoon and wanted to know all about what had occurred at Kerry's house. They had seen it on the news. Kerry told Vin to go and get them and bring them to her place for dinner.

Vin walked them through the cornfields and showed them all the places where there was still blood from the evening before. He showed them where all the vehicles had been on the road and where the drugs had been dropped. And while he did, he routinely looked for more evidence, telling the boys what he was looking for.

They were very impressed, and that was just great.

As Vin walked with them back to the house, he silently thanked a generous lord for the storm clouds just off to the west. One good rain and all the blood and some of the awful memories from the event would simply wash away.

The boys helped walk the beast one more time, and Vin made Kerry and the dog comfortable once again, and then he took the boys home.

On the return, he picked up a lot of beer and some snacks, a change of clothes, some flowers for Kerry, and a pack of hot dogs for the beast and returned to Kerry's crazy house.

She was safe. And Vin was in this for long haul.

CHAPTER 22

When Vin went into the hole for Luke's bills and looked at his urgent situation about needing a structure on his lot before winter came, he decided the best thing to do was park his motor home in one of his father's pole barns for the winter and just move in with his dad until spring.

His father didn't judge him about his overnight absences, and he enjoyed having the boys and Vin full-time every other weekend, so it worked out. And Vin knew he could make the winter chores easier for his father when the snow and ice came and he could take care of the snowplowing.

Vin was comfortable and all set for the time of year when everything just seemed so much harder in Clifton County because of the cold, the snow, and the ice while at the same time giving the folks there three festive holidays, but he could not enjoy the same for Kerry, and he couldn't do anything about it.

In mid-October, Kerry's hours decreased, as so many others had, to twenty-nine hours per week. She was inconsolable.

Even though she knew the decrease was coming, she didn't make enough money to have a cushion in place, and with a daughter at State, there wasn't enough money every month anyway.

Vin thought that the easy solution was to get rid of her house, which probably would have been a fast turnover if she considered all the total strangers who drove down the lane and made her offers.

But he couldn't say anything. Kerry valued her independence, and she had once told him that the reason she did not date many men after the dissolution of her marriage when Elizabeth was only three was that she didn't want anyone telling her what to do.

He could see why men wanted to take care of her. She was sweet and had a wide-eyed philosophy about life, which did not include ever getting hurt or being taken advantage of. She was easy prey, but she seemed to do all right, and Vin was certainly aware that he must never try to take over any part of her life or control her decisions. The few things she let him do for her weren't much, and he didn't ever want to undo his favor with her.

If she had ever been involved with anything that involved his department, things would have been different.

Her immediate loss of income was serious. Kerry got rid of her cable television service, her internet, and her smart phone. She quit using a water conditioner for her bath and laundry water and bought a water pitcher with a filter in it and quit buying bottled water. She bought some craft supplies and planned to make her Christmas gifts. She packed her lunch religiously. She bought nothing at all online because she no longer could. She decreased her weekly trips to Columbus to have lunch or dinner with her daughter to only two a month. She took on extra hours, which still did not give her forty hours per week, at other Well Stores.

But with everything Kerry tried to do for herself, Vin could see that she fell a little further and further into the ditch of debt practically every week. She never mentioned it. He just knew.

They took long walks and attended a few festivals in the area among the blaze of colored leaves that was Ohio in the fall. Even though Vin was not the one out of money, Kerry seemed to want to do things that were free. She even packed a tailgate party when they took the motor home up to Columbus for a whole game day when he would have happily taken her and Elizabeth out for dinner.

She moved her mattress and box springs down to the rarely used dining room and brought her cold weather clothing downstairs too. She told Vin she was not going to use the upstairs for the winter and that she only was going to heat the downstairs.

That was easy enough to do. The house was so big she still had plenty of room in the downstairs. And somewhere in the seventies someone had added a small bath with a shower in the bottom part of the house, so Kerry did not actually need the upstairs.

Vin asked his friend, Charles, to come to the house and help him build a dam, which would keep the warm air from traveling up the staircase and which would swing up against a wall when not in use. As a bonus, Charles brought his wife, Sharon, who was locally famous for her baking skills, and she brought a plate of brownies with her.

Sharon said she had always wanted to see the interior of Kerry's house, so it worked.

Don't encourage her, thought Vin wryly.

He bought Kerry a real featherbed and an electric blanket and told her they were for him.

Together they located and blocked off all the upstairs heating ducts so the warm air would stay on the bottom floor, and they sealed her windows and unused doors with insulating foam.

Vin could not understand why anyone as smart as Kerry would not be able to see the futility of hanging on to a house she could not afford and could not comfortably live in for five months of the year, but he couldn't say a word.

As the cold weather inched closer, Kerry's propane and electric bills shot up dramatically, and the county had started a tax assessment because they thought someday they could bring their over-priced water out to the people who didn't want it.

The first week of November, when Kerry told Vin that she was working extra all weekend, that she had to pick up her niece at the airport on Friday night, and that she felt there would be no time for them to be together, he respected her wishes and took on two shifts at the jail.

She did say she would have breakfast with him the following Monday morning when he invited him. He told her that if that was all he got for three days, he would take it. He didn't really understand why she didn't think they would have time for anything at all, but she told him she actually needed to sleep because the extra work was exhausting.

So when Vin drove to her house on Friday evening just to see if everything was all right while Kerry was at work and saw the candles in the windows and her car parked in its usual spot, he went no farther than her driveway. Then on Saturday at dusk when he again spotted her parked car and saw candles, even in the bathroom window, and saw smoke coming from the grill he had bought her, which meant she was cooking dinner for someone, he almost called her.

He did call her the next morning, but he got no answer. He called again in the afternoon but got the same result.

By Sunday night, when he saw the car, the grill, and the candles again, the only thing he could think was that Kerry had just enjoyed a date for the weekend.

She had told him she was working the evening shifts, which did not end until after ten. And yet her car had been there all three weekend nights.

She had lied to him. Kerry was seeing someone. Whomever she picked up from the airport was staying with her, and whatever they were doing involved lit candles in all the rooms. Apparently, Kerry did not realize that lit candles in her windows were visible from the road.

Vin's blood ran alternately cold and hot. He tried to think of every single reason why she would be at home alone with candles and a cookout, and there simply was no explanation.

And the niece she supposedly picked up at the airport that Friday night obviously was not her niece at all.

He alternated fury and numbness. He couldn't sleep, he couldn't eat, and the prisoners got the brunt of his anger that weekend, not that they noticed.

He intended to pick up Kerry on Monday morning, and he was determined to find out what she was doing to him. To them.

If she had wanted to cool off their relationship a little, or if she wanted it to end for any reason, all she had to do was tell him. If she had wanted to talk about anything at all, he would have been all ears.

Vin felt that he had missed all the warning signs and shifts in his last relationship, and he had been very sensitive to looking for signs of trouble in this one.

There had been none.

CHAPTER 23

Vin showed up as scheduled at eight o'clock Monday morning. Kerry met him on her porch, and she looked as if nothing was amiss.

Vin told her they were going inside, that he needed to talk to her. She seemed surprised or scared. He didn't know what she felt, and he didn't care.

The dog exited as they entered, and it was Vin who closed the door behind them.

"What's wrong?" Kerry said innocently, facing him and looking as sweet as ever.

"Well, why don't you tell me?"

"Tell you what?"

"Well, you could start with the truth."

"Okay, the truth about what? I don't know what you are getting at."

"Come on, Kerry, why don't you just tell me about your romantic weekend visitor?"

Kerry looked absolutely shocked.

"What?" She almost screamed the word.

"I saw the candles, I saw your car, I saw the romantic cookout… Whomever you were with wasn't your niece, and you weren't at work, either."

Kerry folded her arms at her abdomen. She folded over a little. The look on her face was awful.

"How dare you!" she seethed.

"How dare I what? Spy on you? I didn't. You live on a busy street. Everyone can see just about every move you make, including me. And you never answered your phone. Most women trying to cheat on their boyfriends are a little more subtle, don't you think?"

"I don't know. I never cheated on anyone, least of all you," she said calmly.

"Well then, do you want to lie to me some more and try to convince me you were alone all weekend? Be careful… I expose liars for a living!"

Kerry turned away from him. She was trying to decide what to do. Her choices as Vin saw them were somewhere between an explosion and hysteria, and he was prepared for either one.

She surprised him then, went calmly to her kitchen, and picked up some papers by her telephone. She picked up her cell too. She returned to the back room and handed them to him.

"Apparently nothing I say will convince you that I was not lying and am not lying. So here is proof. And I did pick my niece up from the airport Friday night and took her back to her dorm. I only worked half shifts Saturday and yesterday because we weren't busy enough and the stores are trying to cut staff hours, as you already know. And I didn't call you from work because…well, I was embarrassed. I can't pay my bills."

She stood calmly as he glanced at the proffered papers and the nonworking or shut-off phone. Kerry was pale, and she couldn't seem to stand up straight, and she was chewing her lip.

The papers were from the electric company. They had turned off her electricity.

And her phone was disconnected for nonpayment, the same as the electricity was.

He looked at her, a massive apology beginning on his lips.

"So the candles were the only source of light. And I cooked hot dogs all weekend on the grill because I didn't have a stove. And I didn't answer your phone calls because my phone was not working. And I was cold and couldn't bathe in the cold well water with no water heater and the water pump is electric anyway.

"And I didn't tell you all about this because I don't want you to feel sorry for me and I don't want you to pay my bills. None of this was any of your damned business. Everything will be working again on Wednesday, when I get paid."

Then she said the most horrible two words: "Get out!" She jerked her head toward the back door.

"Wait a minute, Kerry." Vin took a step toward her.

She backed away as if he were on fire.

"Kerry, please let me explain!"

"Explain what?" she started to cry and shout at him. Before he could respond, she shouted again. Her shoulders were heaving, and she backed into a wall.

"Explain that I didn't have enough money to pay my bills and so I became a promiscuous whore?"

There was that dreaded term again.

"No, just listen to me!"

"Get out!" she repeated. "Get out or I'll call 911!"

She couldn't do that without a phone. But the point was taken.

Sadly, Vin made his way to the back door, and behind her, he heard her screeching at him. The dog bounded in and planted himself between the two of them and actually bared his teeth at Vin.

The dog barked and barked over her words.

"I loved you! I never ever gave you a single reason to think that there was anyone for me except you! I have been there for you every minute since the night we met! You could have accused me of anything at all and it probably would have been true…except for that!"

He shut the door and went to his truck and couldn't hear her voice anymore, but all the way to the street he heard her pain-filled shrieking in his head.

Then he realized he had nowhere to go. He couldn't see Kerry. He couldn't call her. All he could do was try to make this better.

So he went and bought her a nonplan phone and had it activated with unlimited everything for a month. He drove back to her house and set it on her porch, near the door, with a note that said, "Be safe." His number was already on the phone in case she wanted to call him and yell at him some more.

He called the electric provider and paid her bill, which she had not paid for two months. He stopped at the propane company and prepaid a full tank.

He wanted to do more, but he knew she would not accept anything from him. She had no choice but to let the electricity go back on, and the phone was absolutely necessary since she had no landline.

The county and the city law had the ability to turn on and turn off services when someone was in trouble or someone needed to be flushed out of a property. Had Vin used his brain instead of suspecting Kerry of infidelity, he could have checked to see if her electricity was working on his own duty.

He called his best friend for advice. He was expecting sympathy, but Bitty just told him what an asshole he was.

"Do whatever you have to do to get her back," he said. It sounded like an order.

Then Vin went to the mega Well Store in Warmington and bought Kerry gift cards for gasoline, sandwiches, pizza, and a card to that store so she could buy anything she needed.

He took them to the house with a card that said, "I'm sorry." It had puppies on it.

From that point on, it was up to Kerry. Then all he could do was wait.

He went home and mowed his dad's acreage, which did not actually need to be mowed. But he could scream and shout at himself as the motor was running and the blades were mowing and no one would hear him. It was therapeutic.

So he didn't hear his phone ring, but Kerry had called from the new phone and left a message.

She thanked him. It was very businesslike. She said she would pay him back. She said she didn't know when she would want to talk to him again, but she would let him know.

Then she said the gut-stabbing words, "You hurt me. I never thought you would hurt me," and she hung up.

Vin couldn't do anything else about it. Except to keep trying to let her know he was very wrong and very sorry. He sent roses.

He had lunch with Bitty the next day. He thought he would get some advice, but Bitty railed at him. He told his friend that there were at least a dozen ways Vin could have checked to see what Kerry was up to that weekend, most of them legal.

He said that Vin was a damned suspicious fool, and that he had better keep trying to get Kerry back, because she was everything.

Vin couldn't argue. Then all he could do was wait for her to contact him.

He didn't go near her house while he was on duty because to do so would make him a stalker of sorts. He didn't go near her off duty for the same reason.

He did go fill her gas tank in Hebron one of the days, so he knew she was at work and her car was running. He dropped off a bag of dog food, a bag of rabbit food, and a bunch of carrots with a bow on them at her house when he was sure she was not there.

After a full week, he did not hear from her, so he called and left a message.

"I just wanted to make sure you are all right, Kerry, and tell you that I love you and that I was wrong." He didn't hear from her for the next three weeks. It was torture.

Then it was the middle of November. He renewed the cell phone minutes.

CHAPTER 24

One night when he was on duty and just about ready to head back to the station he got a patched-through call from Warner County. It was a deputy he had worked with on some warrants not long before, and he and his girlfriend had met Kerry and Vin for dinner one evening at the close of the multiple encounters. The deputy told him that a woman he identified as Kerry Court was stranded on the side of the highway and that she said she was waiting for a tow truck. He thought she was lying.

He said she was right on the border of the two counties, about a mile from her house. She didn't want him to wait with her. He thought she might try to walk home and the highway had no sidewalks, as Vin knew. He said he really did not have time to stay with her, she was just about out of his jurisdiction, and he wanted to let Vin know.

Obviously the deputy was speaking in code because he was on duty and using the work phone. He had apparently encountered Kerry, stranded in his county, and she was now walking in Vin's. He wanted Vin to go and fetch her because he wanted to go home.

So Vin called dispatch and told them he was asked to go to a trouble call for assist with a pedestrian on the border. He located Kerry, walking about a quarter mile away from her car, right where the deputy had said she was.

When she saw him, she looked like she wanted to crumble up and blow away, not the greeting he had hoped for.

He pulled up behind her, lights on, which made her shrink away a little more, but that was the policy.

"Hi!" he said, exiting his vehicle and moving toward her. She had lost some weight.

Her face was unreadable.

"Run out of gas or did the car break down?" he asked kindly enough.

"Gas. But I have some at home. In a can left over from my tractor. I can go home and get it. I don't want to bother anybody."

"Get in," he directed more than offered. "I'll take you home, and we can fix this pretty quick."

"I don't want or need your help. I know how to walk. I know where my house is."

Vin shook his head. He went to her side of the cruiser and opened the door.

"Get in," he repeated with less of a jovial ring to his voice. Kerry didn't move.

"If we do this your way, Kerry, I have to cuff you and drag you to the back seat and lock you in. We are in a dangerous position, with the ass of this cruiser sticking halfway into the lane of a highway on a dark night out here. Someone could hit it. Someone could hit us. How about if you just act like an adult here? It is against the law for a pedestrian to walk along a state highway."

It actually was unlawful to walk along a state highway, an interstate. Thankfully she didn't know the law that well.

Kerry started to cry, but she got into the front seat with Vin, which technically was not allowed. She looked defeated, which was not what he intended.

He didn't take her home. He drove to the nearest gas station, took the can from the cruiser, filled it, and drove back to her car. He knew if she actually had gasoline in a can at her house, she would have used it all before she drove to work.

"There," he said when he closed her gas cap. "Get in and turn it on. Sometimes they don't start right up if you have emptied the gas line."

Surprisingly enough, she did what he said. He stood in front of her car so she couldn't take off and leave him in the dust without running him over. She looked like she wanted to. After a couple of tries, the car started right up.

Vin motioned for Kerry to open her window. Then he went to her side of her car.

"Kerry," he said softly, gut-wrenchingly close to her. "If you don't want to be my girlfriend anymore, that is up to you. But I will always care for you. Please don't take risks like this. Just call."

Kerry didn't look at him, and she didn't say anything except a clipped "Thank you." Then she drove off. He followed her home and left her at her driveway. He waited until her saw her kitchen light go on. Then he returned to the station.

Shift over. Another lonely night, but at least he got to see her.

CHAPTER 25

The next morning, Vin woke at dawn, filled his ten-gallon gas can with fuel, and filled the rest of Kerry's gas tank before she even woke up. The dog must have been upstairs with Kerry because Luke did not bark. Vin was jealous of that damned dog, and not for the first time.

Vin never saw the last breath of the beautiful fall, which arrived annually in Clifton County, the fall he had been looking forward to sharing with the beautiful Kerry. Absolutely nothing was pretty to him. It was just getting colder. He had to scrape ice off his windshield in the mornings.

Vin heard that Kerry was working at her uncle's bar in the evenings. That was not necessarily good news. She needed the money, and the money probably was good, but it likely meant she was away from her house and her dog too much and that she was tired all the time.

She had two regular shifts each week, Bitty told her after doing some bar sitting on Vin's behalf. As it turned out, Laura, the pretty, redheaded, full-time barkeep was taking some personal time off. Katherine, Laura's equally pretty but brunette twin and part-timer, who was newly married to Nate, one of the local firefighters, was working full-time, and Kerry was her relief, at least for the holiday season.

When he moved out of his selfish self, Vin thought that maybe Kerry was in a place where she had to at least act like she was having fun. She was around music, a little dancing, people having fun and talking to her, and she was watched over by her uncle.

And that was a far cry from his work alone in a cruiser every day, watching for trouble and bad guys. That autumn Clifton County suffered a rash of adult male suicides, and no matter how many times he was first on the scene of such tragedies, he never got used to it.

New kinds of mixed drug combinations were showing up among the young users, and some of them were deadly. Vin had to appear at more residences in town than usual when called because of suspicious deaths, and a whole new education about what law enforcement was seeing among the users took nearly a month of educational hours away from routine shifts.

He spoke at length to the boys because these killer drugs were permeating even the quiet rural high schools. Bitty gave him permission to take the boys to the county morgue, where they viewed a boy their age who had simply taken a couple of pills at a party and paid for it with his life.

As usual, the facts spoke for themselves. Nothing was more real than a dead body.

CHAPTER 26

Even without her, Vin still considered Kerry to be his girl. He wasn't sure what he was to her.

He worked extra duty, private duty and jail duty, and spent a lot of time at his boys' wrestling matches. He had given one set of State tickets to Bitty and Eileen, and his dad took one grandson at a time to two more games. Vin and Bitty went to a fourth. Vin could not help but have fun, even though he remembered that he had wanted to be with Kerry for at least one last game that season.

Thanksgiving was absolutely the most miserable holiday he had ever spent, even when he first divorced Joan. He worked a double shift just to kill the time.

He drove past Kerry's house routinely as it was still part of his route and saw her and the beast out walking on the lane once and almost stopped by, but he was determined to let her come to him. If she ever did.

The first day of December, a "For Sale" sign went up in front of her house. It bothered Vin. That house meant everything to Kerry, and now she was giving up, he thought. And maybe moving away.

On the other hand, it meant that she might just be moving into a more manageable place in the county.

While he was watching for speeders during one of his shifts, he had an idea that he should call and see if it was possible for him to buy the damned house for her. He was that desperate. But it made no sense, and the end result was not good for Kerry anyway. Because it wasn't just the house payment. It was the taxes, insurance, utilities, maintenance, and everything else she could not afford.

He waited another week to call her, on the phone he was still paying for. It was the least he could do, considering. And he wanted to make sure she had his number handy, always, and could call for help if she needed any, or if she decided to talk to him at all.

He passed Milo's bar regularly during his shifts and whenever he was driving anywhere in Warmington, and he could see that Kerry was working there more frequently than two shifts per week, so he thought her money problems had probably evened out somewhat.

Now it was supposed to be the happiest time of the year, and all he felt was emptiness, a growing frustration with wondering if he would ever be with Kerry again, and he was beginning to think that the answer was no.

He missed her, he missed their times together, he missed seeing her cute little daughter and her big, dumb dog, the dog that had cost him over two thousand dollars, and of course, he missed the warmth and sweetness of her in his arms at night.

He missed her jokes, her teasing, her touch, her smell, the way she tossed her hair and it caught the light and flashed gold streaks, and he missed holding her soft hands with the pretty nails.

He missed her cooking and their talks. He missed everything about her.

As soon as the Christmas lights went on all over the county, Vin felt even worse, knowing without ever having shared them with Kerry that she would be thrilled by all the brightness in the dark.

Kerry was Vin's brightness in the dark. He wished he could tell her.

As Christmas neared, he decided to give the boys cash for a gift to avoid shopping, and for the first time in his career, he did not participate in the Kids 'n' Cops holiday programs. Bitty was still mad at him anyway, and when he didn't sign up for the program, his best friend called him Scrooge.

Vin was miserable.

He almost stopped at Milo's on Christmas Eve, to see Kerry and wish her a Merry Christmas, but he thought better of it. He thought about waiting for her to get off work and escort her home, but if she reacted to his appearance there in a negative way, it might have upset them both.

He spent the rest of the holiday week working, working, and working some more and spending time with his dad and boys when he wasn't working. He spent Christmas Day working, and he stopped in at Bitty's for a quick dinner, not joining in the celebration of anything at all. He just ate. It was Joan's turn to have the boys for Christmas, and Vin's dad had gone to Indiana to be with his sister and her family.

Bitty walked him to his cruiser after the meal and talked to him about Kerry.

"Go see her. Talk to her. Tell her what an asshole you were and make no excuses. I know why you thought she was cheating on you, and I get it, but don't use Joan as an excuse. If she won't talk to you, let me know. I swear I will talk to her myself, at least to make her give you the time to tell her whatever it is you can think up to say. She will listen to me," Bitty finished, and Vin knew that he was right, at least about that.

Vin's father, who could see the sadness in his son and knew full well the reason, only spoke to him about it once. He told Vin that he had to make a permanent decision about Kerry. He advised that it did neither of them any good to leave whatever drove a wedge between them in a state of ongoing indecision.

So Vin decided to go to Milo's on New Year's Eve and talk to Kerry. If she didn't want to see him, that was too bad, she would have to see him one way or another. He would give it one more chance, on the last night of the year, and if she would have nothing to do with him and said that she never would, he would begin the New Year without her. Forever.

CHAPTER 27

Vin worked New Year's Eve day, went home and showered, put on the new sweater the boys gave him for Christmas via Joan, and drove to Milo's. He called his sons from the parking lot to see what they were doing for night and told them to be good. He told his dad he might not be home until late, if at all, and wished him a Happy New Year.

A big snow was scheduled to hit that evening and continue overnight, and Bitty felt that the drinkers would be heading home early or just not go out at all. And if they did drink too much and it snowed, they would be easy enough to catch because of the slide-offs.

Even then, all the deputies were on call, including those who, like Vin, had worked the day shift already and who might be scheduled for the next day too, which Vin was not.

He was happy to see there were not many patrons lingering at Milo's that night. He located Kerry's car and parked right next to it.

Then he took a deep breath, stepped inside the double-door entry, and was immediately accosted by Kerry's Uncle Tony.

"There you are, Deputy!" he said with his husky, juicy voice, and he slammed his meaty fist down on Vin's shoulder like he always did. He acted as if he was expecting him.

"I've been wondering where you have been. How come you haven't been coming in here to see my best bartender, eh?"

As usual, Tony did not let Vin speak, he just continued, uninterrupted.

"I figure either you don't like her working here, or you two have had some sort of blowout, am I right? I see her… I watch my niece… known her since she was born. I see her look up every time someone comes through the door, and she looks disappointed because it's never you. Sometimes, certain songs play on the juke, and I see her crying into the beer coolers, see? Like maybe that was one of your special songs together, am I right?"

He jabbed Vin in the chest. "Tell you what, Deputy, how about I give you a break here? How about I ask you to stay and close the place up tonight and make sure Kerry gets out of here all right, eh? I'll tell her the way it is. She won't dare argue with me, see? It works both ways… Maybe you will get a little, and I know if I show up early tonight, maybe I will get a little from my wife, too, see? Hell, it's practically a holiday. Everybody should be getting a little, eh Deputy?"

Vin found it a bit unsettling that Kerry's uncle thought that Vin having sex with her tonight would be a perfectly good thing. Most fathers and uncles considered their young female relatives virgins until death.

"And then, after she puts the money away, you talk to her. Don't let the year end with whatever you did or she did to cause you two to break up, got it? Don't let her walk out this door without a resolution, got it? A New Year's resolution."

Then he punched Vin in the shoulder and walked back into the bar.

He never gave Vin a chance to accept or decline his proposal, but it actually sounded like a good idea. As he made his way into the dark bar, still festooned with colored Christmas lights, he could see Tony explaining to Kerry that she was going to have help to close. She looked at Vin briefly, argued just a little, and then shook her head as she lost the argument, as did everyone who challenged Tony.

Vin hung up his leather jacket and took the last seat at the bar where he could see one television screen and nearly every table in the place, and then he texted Bitty that he was the security at Milo's for the duration.

Within seconds, a text came back from Bitty.

"Good luck," it said. "Get it done."

A beer appeared so quickly that he did not even see Kerry deposit it in front of him. If he wanted something else, he was out of luck, he thought. She didn't look at him again for a long time, but it didn't matter because he could finally look at her all evening and she couldn't do a thing about it.

She looked beautiful. She was wearing a light-blue short-sleeved sweater that was studded with pearls all over the front. She had a gold chain with a single pearl dangling from it, and the pearl played pcekaboo with her cleavage as she dashed here and there efficiently around the bar.

Every time she bent down to wash glasses or reach for a beer deep inside the cooler, her breasts swelled dangerously close to the neckline of the sweater, but he knew her well enough to know that she had not intended such a show.

She was wearing little pearl drop earrings with something shiny on them, earrings that danced with her hair and her laughter as she interacted with the patrons, who were mostly male.

She laughed with the servers as they came to the service end where they ordered and picked up their customer's drinks. She washed glasses and set them atop the various levels of shelving to dry, and she wiped the bar down with a towel when someone left. She worked the small space professionally and efficiently. If she was shaken by Vin being in close proximity, she did not show it to the others.

Her uncle was right. When a song they had enjoyed together came on the jukebox, her eyes got wet. Just a little, and she hid it by acting like she was rearranging a cooler.

But when Vin set his empty bottle on the refill shelf, she sent a fresh one careening toward him instead of bringing it to him, and if he hadn't seen it, he would have been covered with cold beer and broken glass.

Maybe, he thought, she intended it that way. He ignored the act.

CHAPTER 28

The night moved quickly toward the early last call due to the nature of the holiday. The patrons left one by one, some of them leaving larger bills on the bar for Kerry and leaning over for a quick peck on her cheek.

She must have wished everyone but him a "Happy New Year!" fifty times. She started to let the servers off one by one after she closed the kitchen.

When the bar was nearly empty, she came to Vin and told him that he did not have to stay.

"I've got this," she offered stubbornly.

Vin smiled at her.

"I'm not leaving until you do," he said.

Kerry actually hissed at him, knowing that he wasn't going anywhere no matter what she said or did. So she decided to just ignore him. She was good at that part.

When there were only a couple of guys left at the bar, Vin went to check out the parking lot. At least four inches of fresh snow had fallen silently since he went into Milo's earlier in the evening. It was still coming down, large flakes that piled on to the depth already there. The parking lot was a mess, and he did not see any sign of plows on the roads yet.

So Kerry wasn't driving home, either. When he had her imprisoned in his truck, she would have to listen to him.

When Kerry walked the last lone patron to the exit, Vin waited for the sound that she had locked both entry doors, and then he relaxed a little.

She continued to ignore him as she wiped down the bar once more, emptied the sinks, turned off the outside lights, and cleared out the register. She took the money to the back of the building, and then Vin went into action.

He checked the front doors, the restrooms, the whole floor, and he went to the kitchen. He checked the kitchen door and the other back door, not speaking to the girl counting money and entering figures onto a tally sheet, who acted as if he was not there at all.

Then he went to the front room and sighed, thinking there was nothing quite as nice as a bar with no one in it, which made no sense. But it was dark except for the last night of the Christmas lights and the glow of the jukebox, and then he had an idea.

He located the song Kerry was playing when he first met her that spring, and he added the song he suggested she play when he first approached her. In the empty bar, she would hear them from the kitchen.

In a perfect world, Vin thought, Kerry would have come out to him, held her arms up to dance, and they would have spent the rest of their lives in each other's arms. No words would have been necessary at all.

But in the real world, Kerry did exit the kitchen, but she went to the bar and gathered up the dirty towels instead. She stopped at the jukebox, pressed a code for a free play, located the number for a particularly snarky song about a girl getting revenge upon a guy, turned the volume up, then she went back through the swinging doors, leaving Vin in the proverbial dust.

Vin sighed. Nothing about this, he thought, was going to be easy. He saw the kitchen go dark.

Kerry came back to the barroom with her coat. She didn't have anything to do or anything to say, so she just said, "Let's go."

"Not so fast," Vin said. "We need to talk." He could see her fingers fidgeting with the hem of her sweater.

"I don't want to talk. I want to go home. There is nothing to say," she said without looking at him.

He pulled out a chair at a table in the center of the space and gestured to her to take it. She already knew there was no argument with this.

Vin had always wondered why Kerry never tested him on the "I'm bigger than you" things. He thought maybe it was because he was a deputy and she already knew she would not win, but in reality, she had nothing to fear. He never would have laid a forceful hand upon her.

"Okay, I'll give you a couple of minutes," she said, taking the seat. "Your boss said I had to listen to you, but he didn't say for how long. There is something I want first."

"What? Anything," he said, and he meant that. So Bitty had contacted her as he had said he would.

"I want a beer. I am too tired, and my feet hurt too damned much to get it myself."

"Done," Vin said hopefully. He went to the coolers, withdrew two beers, and grabbed a glass. He put a wad of bills on the register, not having any idea how much he was paying, and he did not care.

He returned to the table, twisted off the tops, and gave Kerry her beer and her glass. Then he sat down across from her again.

The muffled sound of fireworks and car and truck horns blared outside just then as the clock apparently struck midnight. Vin hoped he did not hear gunfire.

"Happy New Year, Kerry," he said softly.

"You too." She sounded like she meant it.

He started to speak. He had made a mental outline, and he followed it pretty well, considering all the feedback he was getting from Kerry was a look of boredom.

He told her that he had been wrong, that he had been an idiot, that he could have checked to see why her lights were actually out that night but he had been too blinded by the falsehood that jumped into his mind. He told her that if it had not been her house, he would have called and checked as a routine gesture, but for some reason, he didn't think about it. He was so upset by what he thought he saw.

He went on to say that she had never given him any reason at all to think that she was cheating or even thinking about it, and he called himself a few more names.

Kerry wasn't bailing him out. She finished her beer quickly and waved the bottle at him.

"Sure," he said as she kicked off her shoes and put her feet up on another chair. Vin went to the cooler, got her another beer, and unrolled some more bills and left them on the register. He might have been leaving a hundred dollars there for the next opener, and if he was, he did not care.

He waited then. He waited for Kerry to start on the second beer and maybe think about what he was saying. Vin was beginning to feel a tiny sliver of encouragement.

After a long enough pause, he started to grovel. He told her it would never happen again. He told her that if he ever had a question, he would just ask. He told her his life was miserable without her, and that if she did not reconsider, he understood, and that after tonight, he would never bother her again, but that if she ever needed anything, he hoped she would call because what they had shared would not end with a breakup, that he would always love her.

He said there would never be another woman for him. That she was it.

Then he stopped. He had nothing else. Nothing.

Kerry looked at her toes, wiggled them, winced a little, and looked at her hands to see what the night had done to her manicure, and she sighed.

Then she put her bare feet back on the floor and turned her chair back so her legs were under the table, and she poured the rest of her beer into her glass.

She chugged it and sort of slammed the glass back onto the table.

Then she looked squarely at Vin, shrugged her shoulders as if she could not have cared less, and said, "Okay."

She certainly got his attention.

"Okay what?" he asked her softly.

Kerry actually yawned. He heard her shuffle her shoes on the floor as she put her feet back into them.

"Okay to everything. Can I go now? Can we go now?" she corrected herself.

"Wait," Vin remained frozen in place, dumbfounded. "You mean, we are back together? You mean you will take me back?"

Kerry looked at him and smiled sweetly.

"I already did. I was going to call you tonight and tell you, but you beat me to it. Besides, it was so much fun to see you scared of me and hear you grovel that I decided to wait until just now—"

Her last remark was cut off and punctuated with a shriek. Vin jumped up and was around the table and behind her in a flash. He lifted her chair off the floor and spun the chair with Kerry in it around and around until Kerry laughed so hard she screamed she was going to throw up.

She was still laughing when he set the chair on top of the table so she could not get out of it without his help.

"Nice" was all he said to her.

"Let's go!" was all she said to him. He took her elbows and forearms and lifted her back to the floor. He replaced the chair.

It was wonderful to touch her. And then he could not feel his feet touching the wooden floor just like the first night he approached her at the jukebox and she agreed to join him for a drink.

Kerry put on her coat, and Vin went to the bar and got his. He made one more round of the building, checked the safe, and made sure the lights were out, and he found Kerry waiting by the front door for him.

Waiting. For him. She was a beautiful sight. Vin's heart jumped a little.

"Have you looked outside?" he said. She shook her head.

Then he opened the door. Kerry gasped at the way the parking lot had transformed while she worked.

"It's beautiful!" she said and stepped out from under the overhang. Then she put her head back, opened her mouth, and tried to catch a snowflake or two.

Vin saw that as an invitation. He wrapped her up in his arms and kissed her until she started to shiver, and he hoped it wasn't from the cold.

"You can't drive home in this," he told her.

She opened her mouth to protest, and he kissed her again. Then he swept her up in his arms and carried her to his truck and unlocked the door. She got inside, but then she stepped back out again and acted like she was brushing snow off the windshield with her mitten.

Actually, she was making a snowball. When Vin reached into the back of the cab for his long-handled snow-removal brush, she lofted it over the top of the truck. It made a direct hit on the back of his head, and the cold snow went right down the back of his neck and melted into his collar and sweater.

"Oops!" Kerry giggled.

Vin did not react. He would get her later, when he got her home safely, when they were out in the middle of nowhere and no one would hear her scream. He owed her something like that since she had tortured him all night for no reason.

The first snowplow drove by them in the direction of Kerry's house just as they were about to exit the parking lot.

"Perfect!" Vin said. Then he looked at Kerry, seated next to him where he had wanted her to be for these awful past months.

"You are perfect, too," he said tenderly. She smiled at him and said nothing.

Vin simply followed the plow to Kerry's long driveway. He drove down it just fast enough that the tires did not get mired in the deepening snow.

When he pulled behind the house instead of next to it so that the truck would be protected from the heavy part of the snowfall, Kerry exited the truck and ran to the house for the dog.

So Vin was accosted for a second time. The beast was so happy to see him that he cried and whimpered and ran around him in circles when he wasn't trying to jump onto his shoulders.

Finally he bounded off toward the barren fields, and Kerry stood on the porch and looked at Vin.

"Come here and look at this moon," he called softly to her. So she descended the two steps off the porch and took a step toward him.

Vin moved toward Kerry like a shot. He picked her up, tossed her into a snowbank, and rolled with her in the snow. He shoved some down the front of her sweater. He would have buried her, but she was screaming so much he quit as he saw Luke bounding toward them to see what Kerry was screaming about.

She stood up, said some very un-Kerry-like words, and stomped into the house.

Vin made it to the door before she could slam it and lock him out.

Inside, he immediately went for the woodstove. He had a pretty good flame going before Kerry even had all of her wet outerwear off.

Vin removed his leather jacket.

While he was building the fire to get some added heat into the damned place, he started to wonder if Kerry wanted him to stay. He resolved to let her take all the next steps.

When he stood up and looked at her, she was standing with only the night-light of the kitchen behind her and the open flame in the stove illuminated her with a soft golden glow, and she was gazing at Vin with a look he had never mistaken.

Then she peeled off her wet sweater.

That was all it took.